Bluey's Café

By Veronika Sophia Robinson

Starflower Press

Bluey's Café
© Veronika Sophia Robinson
© Cover illustration by Sara Simon
© Lyrics to Red Dirt and Bouncing Babies by Mandy Bingham
ISBN 978-0-9575371-2-5
Published by Starflower Press, November 2013
www.starflowerpress.com
British Library Cataloguing in Publication Data.
A catalogue record for this book is available from the
British Library.

Other books by the same author:

Fiction
Fields of Lavender (poetry) 1991 ~ out of print
Mosaic 2013
Blue Jeans 2014 ~ illustrated children's book

Non-fiction
*The Compassionate Years ~ history of the Royal New Zealand
Society for the Protection of Animals*, RNZSPCA 1993
*The Drinks Are On Me: everything your mother never told you
about breastfeeding* (First edition published by Art of Change
2007) (Second edition by Starflower Press 2008)
Allattare Secondo Natura (Italian translation of The Drinks Are
On Me 2009) published by Terra Nuova
www.terranuovaedizioni.it
The Birthkeepers: reclaiming an ancient tradition (2008)
*Stretch Marks: selected articles from The Mother magazine 2002 –
2009*, co-edited with Paul Robinson
Life Without School: the quiet revolution (2010),
co-authored by Paul, Bethany and Eliza Robinson
*The Nurtured Family: ten threads of nurturing to weave through
family life* (2011)
Natural Approaches to Healing Adrenal Fatigue (2011)
*The Mystic Cookfire: the sacred art of creating food for friends and
family* (more than 260 vegetarian recipes) (2011)
The Blessingway: creating a beautiful Blessingway ceremony
(2012)
Baby Names Inspired by Mother Nature (2012)

For
René and Chantal

May you always believe in each other.

VSR

Leaving

'You were always more than enough for me, Bluey. You have to know that. You have to know that you made my life,' Emily Miller gasped through her final words, hand in hand with her only child. But her hands weren't the softly moisturised ones with immaculately painted nails that Bluey had known for almost three decades. These hands were poor imposters: pale, bruised and limp. The real Emily Miller's hands were beautiful and ladylike, but frail hands took up residence, and refused to leave.

Bluey spoke gently. 'I love you, Mother. You were always more than enough for me, too. More than enough.'

Tears trickled, but they had nowhere to go and no-one to witness them. 'Thank you for everything.'

Her mother passed away quietly, several hours later, when all her bodily systems had finally shut down. Emily Miller's death wouldn't make the world news, but her life had been the whole world to Bluey.

She wanted to shout from the hospice rooftop that her mother was gone; to tell the whole world that her heart had been torn apart and that her life would never, could never, be the same again.

Bluey was alone now. There was no family left. No mother, no father, no brothers or sisters. This was it: the end of the line. It had always been just the two of them: *the Miller duet*, they called themselves. And now she was one. Bluey wasn't sure she knew how to play a solo part. For as long as she could remember, Emily Miller was by her side cheering her on. Mother, best friend, playmate. Emily Miller was everything to her. Bluey nodded solemnly as the on-duty nurse came into the room. A simple bodily movement to indicate that her mother had gone. A life well lived, now over. Expired.

Emily was finally at peace after weeks of rapid decline.

'Are you okay?' the woman in a white starched

uniform asked with tenderness and care, as she took note of the time of death: 11.20am.

'Not really, no. I've had months to prepare for this moment and I'm not prepared at all,' she cried. 'What am I supposed to do now? How do I walk away? How do I leave her? What happens to her now?'

Bluey sobbed into the nurse's arms. She could smell the pine-forest-scented deodorant, and the fragrance of the fabric conditioner on her uniform: white lily. It was all too much information to take in. The only thing she wanted to think about was her mother. She didn't need sensory overload right now. Bluey pulled away, wanting to retain her own space. No deodorant, no fabric conditioner, no hairspray.

'I'll get you a cup of tea, and then the chaplain will come, if you like. Her body will be looked after in the morgue, and you'll need to make arrangements with the funeral director. There's only one of those in Calico Bay. No choice, I'm afraid. If you need any help or support, the hospital counsellor can guide you.'

The elderly nurse headed off to the staff kitchen to make them both a cup of tea. When she returned, she pulled up a chair by Bluey's side and shared how she came to be a hospice nurse.

'When my mother died, it helped me to really understand my own mortality, and although I witness death every day, in a strange way it has helped me to really value my own life. People come to meet the face of death in so many different ways. Some, like your mother,' she said, gently touching Bluey's hand, 'do it with clarity, fearlessness and grace. That's pretty rare, and it really says a lot about who she was as a person.'

'Yeah, she was pretty amazing,' Bluey smiled, recognising that her mother was still teaching her right up until the last moment. She slowly sipped her strong, steaming tea, then, after touching her mother's hand one last time, headed down the hallway to make a phone call.

'Olivia, can you shut the café and come and get me?' Bluey wailed down the phone. 'Mum's gone. I'm in no state to drive.'

'Honey, I'm so sorry. I'll be straight there.'

They'd been best friends since grade one, and had been inseparable. *Twins separated at birth*, they often said.

Olivia shooed the customers in Bluey's Café onto the verandah, as they dragged their lattes and cappuccinos out the front door. The news that Emily Miller was dead shocked them all. They shouldn't have been shocked: they all knew it was just a matter of time. Olivia locked the door, and left the customers stranded on the front verandah, like a pod of beached whales. They congregated in one corner, taking in the shocking news. The bay wouldn't be the same without the woman who mended their clothes and sewed the finest wedding dresses for fifty kilometres.

Within ten minutes, Olivia was by Bluey's side at the front entrance of the hospice, hugging, consoling and holding.

'You'll get through this. You're not as alone as you think you are. You've got so many people who love you,' Olivia said kindly. 'I know they're not your mum, but they care for you so much. They're family, too, you know. You mustn't doubt that. Lean on us. That's what friends are for, okay?'

'Olivia, it just feels wrong to leave her here in the care of strangers,' Bluey whispered, rubbing her eyes from exhaustion.

'I know,' she said, thoughtfully. 'There are other options, such as home care of the body, but generally that's something you'd think of in advance. Did you and your mum talk of funeral plans?' Olivia asked.

'A while back we did. To be honest, I was too busy caring for her to give much thought to what would happen later,' she sighed. 'She did mention something about being buried in a willow coffin. I've got a feeling, if memory serves me correctly, that she's already paid for a plot somewhere. I don't know. I can't remember right now. I guess it will be in her paperwork. She told me yesterday that I need to look in the top drawer of her dresser. I assume that's what she meant. Can you take me home now?' she pleaded. 'I'm so tired and I've got a headache.'

Olivia drove the back roads from the hospice to Bluey's home. The midday Sun was scorching, and when they arrived they took shelter on the well-shaded verandah.

'Sit down, Bluey. I'll go and grab us some water.' Olivia headed to the kitchen. She knew how hard this was going to be on her friend, and that the next few months would be especially challenging. They spent the afternoon talking about Bluey's memories of Emily, and all the things that made her laugh and cry: a mother-and-daughter relationship based on love and friendship.

Olivia said, 'I've never known a mother and daughter to have a bond like you two had. It truly was remarkable.' She gave her another hug. Bluey was going to need a lot of them if she was to make it through the days ahead.

'I suppose I had better go and phone the funeral director,' Bluey said, resignedly. 'It's all starting to feel a bit real now.'

'I can stay the night, you know. It's no problem.' Olivia said, offering her unconditional support. 'I can phone Hexham now and let him know I'm staying over.'

'Thank you, but I think I'll spend some time on my own. It's a bit hard grieving in a hospital room. I need to have the space to start doing that, but thank you.'

Olivia drove home, and Bluey reluctantly went inside the house she'd shared with her mother for almost three decades. The rooms were all the same as when she was here this morning at 5am, but something had changed. It was no longer their home; it was Bluey's home. At some point she'd have to let go of her mother's personal belongings. Not today though, and not next week, either. She promised herself that she'd do it when she was ready, not when the calendar called out "enough is enough". Most people would have left their family home years before, and headed off to the Big Smoke, or travelled the world for a year or two. Not Bluey. She loved living at home, and she thrived on the relationship she'd had with her mother. Her whole life was in Calico Bay. There was plenty of space for them both to pad around the house without getting under each other's feet.

'Calico Bay Funeral Home, Jenna speaking; how may I help you?' the kind voice asked down the phone line.

'My name's Bluey Miller. I need to make arrangements for my mother's body.' And the words which started to come out so matter of factly became a jumbled cry down the phone line.

Jenna waited patiently. 'Take your time,' was all she said. 'There's no hurry. Just take your time.' She was used to people dissolving on her: an occupational hazard. Death of a loved one brought up people's deepest emotions. It often rendered them inarticulate.

Jenna offered to send one of their staff to come to Bluey's home the following morning.

'Thank you,' she said, and sat on the sofa to cry.

At 9am, Jeff Morimando arrived, dressed in his black and white suit. 'Bluey Miller?' he asked as she opened the stained-glass front door.

Bluey nodded. She dared not speak. Tears were close by, waiting to enter from stage left. They just needed her cue. Instead, she directed Mr Morimando to the lounge, and they sat on the sofas. There were two lime-green linen sofas in that room, both covered in fabric chosen by Emily Miller. She was still there. Her memory was everywhere. Bluey poured Jeff a glass of water and offered him a biscuit.

'I'm sorry for your loss,' he said kindly; and he spoke as if he really meant it. She could tell that although he was new to his job in Calico Bay, he was skilled in this situation, but also that he didn't do it by rote. Bluey's story of loss was as unique to him as it was to her.

'You should know that your mother has already paid for her funeral, and that she had things set in place so you wouldn't have to be too concerned with arrangements. Did she tell you this?' he asked, brushing his fingers through his sandy blonde hair. He suspected that Bluey didn't know too much at all about her mother's plans.

'She said something about a willow coffin, but to be honest, her funeral wasn't uppermost in my mind at the time. I was just hoping she'd live,' Bluey reflected, her long, honey-blonde hair falling over her shoulders, as she cast her eyes to the floor.

'I see. Well, let me talk you through it. Emily bought a small piece of land from behind your café. Did you know that?' he asked, feeling too wary of dropping any big bombshells.

'Really? Are you sure?' Bluey thought he must have confused her mum with someone else. 'She didn't say a word. Mother didn't keep secrets from me. We shared everything. She would have told me!' Bluey was directing her frustration at the stranger, even though she knew it wasn't his fault or responsibility.

'I'm sorry Miss Miller. I guess she was trying to make your life a bit easier. She bought two acres of land from Pen Grille. He owns the 200 acres of land behind your café.'

'I know who Pen is! He's a dear friend of my family. My mother bought the building my café is in from him. I just don't understand how she didn't tell me this.'

'The two acres of land is the strip of eucalyptus trees by Bendigo Creek. Your mother instructed us that she wanted to be buried there. And Emily's friend, Nadia? Although she's a marriage celebrant, she's agreed to officiate the ceremony.' His words were gentle. He wanted to ease Bluey into this pre-arranged funeral plan as easily and kindly as possible. He could see she was still deep in shock, not just from her mother's passing the day before, but from this secret plan Emily had hatched.

'So is there anything I need to do or has my mother covered everything?' Bluey couldn't help letting out a laugh as she fiddled with the hem of her orange T-shirt. 'She was always taking care of me, and even now that I'm 29 years old she's still doing it. Even when she's dead, she's still looking after me!' She shook her head, and could finally see the funny side.

You were always enough for me. Her mother's dying words came back to her, and suddenly the laughter which came up from nowhere vanished like a magician's rabbit and was replaced by deep, gut-wrenching sobs.

He let her cry for a while, and offered her his clean handkerchief.

'Miss Miller, you do have to do some things, though. You need to decide on what day the burial will be, and you need to call friends and family. Can you do that?' he asked. 'I understand from Nadia that she's arranged for the reception to be held near the grave site, just by the creek. I believe that all the food and drinks have been organised, and that a small gazebo will be put up for the day. Cars will need to be parked on the road by the café, though, and people will have to walk up the dirt track to get there. I hope that's okay?'

'Yes, yes, of course it is.'

She'd hardly given her café much thought in recent weeks. Bluey had left the day-to-day running of it in Olivia's capable hands.

'Let's make it for Wednesday afternoon. Is that okay? I'll make calls today,' she sniffed, but her thoughts were elsewhere now. She needed to cook. This is what would help her through these next days, weeks and months.

Bluey guided him to the front door, grabbed her keys, and got on her red scooter to ride to the café.

Bluey's Café

It had been about two weeks since Bluey last stepped in the café. She'd spent every day by her mother's bedside, sharing stories, reminding each other of all their wonderful memories. At night, Bluey came home, too exhausted to think, and slept soundly till first light, and then returned to the hospice room which had been her mother's final home.

It felt so good to be back here in Bluey's Café. The smell of cinnamon and banana muffins greeted her first. The wooden floor hadn't long been mopped. Olivia must be somewhere nearby, she thought. The shop was due to open at 10am, but she found the double glass front doors already unlocked and opened wide to let in the sea air.

Bluey stood there, taking in the calm of Calico Bay. It was named after the unbleached, unprocessed cotton made by traditional Indian weavers. The sand resembled the fabric in colour and texture; unseparated husks, here and there.

This was the only home she'd ever known. Some of her strongest memories were played out within a five-kilometre radius. Her childhood days were spent running up and down the beach with her mother, having sandcastle competitions, and dressing her shelldolls in seaweed. They were good days. *The best days.*

Most mornings, the café opened at 7am for the breakfast crowd, but on Saturdays it opened at 10am for brunch. Bluey looked over today's chalkboard menu:

Sweet potato and ginger tagine
Red capsicum stuffed with olives and black quinoa,
in a ratatouille sauce
Field mushrooms on ciabatta
Pineapple sponge cake
Forest-berry crumble

Bluey realised she hadn't eaten a proper meal in weeks. Her tummy rumbled as she breathed in the smell of mushrooms simmering in olive oil. Now it was time to think about herself. Olivia walked in through the back door, having just emptied the mop bucket.

'Hey Bluey, what are you doing here?' she said, concern coming through every word. 'You don't have to come back yet. Take all the time you need,' she insisted. 'I can manage this place on my own for a bit longer, you know.'

'I just needed to be somewhere familiar for a while. The house is so empty without Mum. It's just not the same. So, so empty. I can't bear it,' she wept, wiping her eyes, then looking up like a hungry dog, she said 'Olivia, it smells so good in here.'

'Have you eaten breakfast?' Olivia asked, putting the mop and empty bucket in a cupboard.

'No, and I'm starving.'

'Sit down, and I'll bring you some brekkie.'

Ten minutes later, Olivia arrived with a plate of grilled tomatoes, homemade pesto, field mushrooms and char-grilled tofu. 'Eat that, and I'll get the outside tables and chairs set up on the verandah. I need to open in ten minutes.'

Bluey had forgotten how good the food in her café was, and ate through the whole meal like a starving refugee.

'Blimey, girl, you are hungry!' Olivia said, astonished at the speed with which Bluey had eaten. 'Look, do you really want to be out here when I open up? Wouldn't you prefer to be in the kitchen or out the back garden?'

'Yeah, I'll go out the back. Thanks Olivia,' she said, touching her friend's hand. 'Thanks for looking after me.' They hugged for a while, and then Bluey headed off to the kitchen, pottering about, unpacking produce and placing fruits and vegetables into wicker baskets, and herbs into glass jars filled with water.

The morning crowd arrived bang on ten, ready for their top three: coffee, newspaper and muffin. Olivia was flat out for at least an hour, and then Bluey popped her head around and said, 'Shall I help you?'

'Can you? It's manic today,' Olivia replied, grateful for the relief after all. The last few weeks had been tough on her, managing the café on her own, day in and day out. She was utterly exhausted, and Bluey could see that in the purple bags under Olivia's eyes.

'Bluey, you're back? I'm ever so sorry to hear about your mum. I really am. If there's anything I can do, let me know,' offered Ivan Bourke, the local postman, who stopped by at the same time every day for his morning break. He was six feet three inches, and had a shock of spiky silver hair, and over-the-top moustache. It was Bluey's Café, and Bluey's tender care and food, which helped Ivan through his divorce and on the road to new love. Bluey liked to think she offered a seaside matchmaking service, even if her own track record was bad advertising. She could see in his blue eyes that he was genuinely concerned for her.

'Thanks Ivan, I'm bearing up.' She felt her heart as heavy as lead. Bearing up? Who was she kidding? This is what it was going to feel like each and every time she came across someone for the next little while.

Suzanne and Felicity, the local aerobics instructors, came up to the counter, head to toe in hot pink lycra, bleach-blonde bobs swishing, and leant over to whisper, 'Bluey, we were so sad to hear about your loss. You have our deepest sympathies. Your mum was a great woman.'

And so it went on, all day. How could people not express their kindness and condolences? Bluey was part of their everyday life. She didn't just serve up muffins and coffee, she served up love and vivaciousness. Her joy for life was utterly contagious, and people wanted some of that. They got it in bucket loads, by osmosis: just by being in the same room as her. Her childlike almond eyes and beaming smile brought sunshine to everyone's day. And now, her sunshine was hidden by an expanse of grey cloud, hovering like it had no intention of ever leaving.

It was as hard for her customers as it was for her. Her natural enthusiasm and boundless energy for life was in the midst of a thunderstorm. She had to take cover.

'Olivia, I'm going to head home now,' she said at three o'clock. This was their usual closing time anyway, but she didn't have the energy to stay behind and clean up.

'No problem. Please don't feel you have to come in on Monday. And it goes without saying that the café will be shut on Wednesday,' Olivia said firmly.

Grabbing her keys, Bluey headed outside and sat on her scooter. She didn't ride straight home, but took the lane up to the edge of the creek where her mother wanted to be buried. Bluey stood there, in the afternoon sunshine, taking in the sounds of kookaburras in gum trees, and crows crawing. A noisy rosella, adorned in bright colours of red, yellow, green and blue, was making a rapid, high-pitched call: *pi pi pi pi pi.*

She closed her eyes, and sighed deeply. Breathing the earthy scent of the scrubland floor beneath her, she unashamedly let the tears fall onto the dry red soil. The scent of the eucalyptus leaves underfoot reminded her of the reason she was here: Emily.

Her mother had been so thoughtful. She knew that Bluey wouldn't want to be in an anonymous church or hall for the final goodbye, but out in the arms of nature. They'd spent many times walking along this part of the creek, and enjoying the tranquillity of the bushland setting. This resting place was where she wanted to be, and it felt right to be here.

Bluey thought about her life here, and what this land meant to both of them; how the landscape captures your imagination, and before you know it, you've fallen in love with everything: the red soil, dry grasses, stones glinting in the harsh sunlight. She recalled their love of the Autumn sunsets, and the amber skies across the bay, and how the red earth transformed to purple with the blossoms of millions of flowers after the rain.

To Bluey, Bendigo Creek was a spectacular place, lined with eucalyptus trees. The whispering wind carried the soulful cry of the storm bird on cool clear nights, and stars shimmered overhead; the earth under her bare toes, a balm to pain.

There was no better smell in the world than eucalyptus after the rain. The Australian bush was her home; the scantily clad foliage of eucalyptus trees and their peeling bark, imprinted upon her memories of childhood. To Bluey Miller, the smells of Australia were simple: horse manure, wind, bushfires, eucalyptus.

The Black Gates

Bluey was folding away her clothes when she suddenly remembered her mother's instruction to look in her drawer. Bluey hadn't planned to go in her mother's bedroom for some time, but she found herself standing by the pine dresser, hesitating for a few moments, and then opening the drawer. It felt so intrusive. There was paperwork confirming her mother's funeral plans, and some jewellery and personal mementos and a book. On the cover, was a yellow Post-It note in Emily's handwriting: *For Bluey.* She picked it up, wondering what it could be. It was thick, like the Oxford English Dictionary, and weighed heavy as a brick. 'What is this?' she asked herself out loud, and carried it to her mother's bed.

Dear diary...
Today is the beginning of the rest of my life. I'm 29 years old, and my life will never be the same again.

That's funny, Bluey thought. *That's the same age as I am now.* She continued to read.

I made my usual walk from the town car park in Rallervale to Hannah's Dress Shop to deliver the latest clothing I'd made, when I slowed down by the old orphanage on Oak Tree Lane. The children were all at play, running across the field, climbing the oak trees, laughing and screaming. All the children, that is, except one little girl. She stood at the black, wrought-iron gates with her little, chubby, dimpled fingers wrapped firmly around two poles. In one hand, was a little blue blanket that she hung onto for dear life. Blonde hair tousled around her shoulders, and she looked up at me and asked 'Will you be my mummy?'

I couldn't move. I froze. She was barely three years old. How could I say 'No, I'm not your mummy'? How could I say 'You don't have a mummy. You're an orphan.'? My heart broke in two. This beautiful little child looked up at me with big almond eyes and a smile to melt my heart. How was I going to walk away? I didn't dare break her heart. It was enough that mine was breaking. How could such a beautiful child be all alone in the world? I told her I had to go, and I walked away carrying my bag of home-made clothing. Turning my back on her was the hardest thing I've ever had to do in my life. I didn't dare look back. By the time I'd arrived at Hannah's, I was in such a state. Hannah took the clothes, and sat me down. Half an hour later, I was inside the orphanage making arrangements to become that little girl's mother. It wasn't an easy process. I was a single woman. I had no experience with children. I'd never even babysat for my friends! The only thing I had going for me, in their eyes, was that I had a reliable self-employed income. But I persisted.

One month later...I've been there every day trying to cut their red tape. Most of the time they're tying it in knots around my heart. They've agreed to let me foster for six months, on a trial. I knew, though, that once we walked out the door, we'd never be parted. I'd make sure of that!

Mama's Bed

Bluey always knew she'd been adopted. That had never been a secret. But she'd never read these words, or heard this story before. Her mother had said that she would only ever adopt a child if the parents were dead. The version of adoption that Bluey knew involved it being a well thought-out plan.

She sat on the bed sobbing for some time. The thought of herself, with her little blue blanket, standing at the orphanage gates asking Emily to be her mother was too much for her to read. Tears chucked themselves convulsively from her body, like an ancient exorcism rite, choking her up, reminding Bluey of all she had lost when Emily died, and all she had gained by being adopted.

Her biological parents had been killed in a car accident a few months before she was taken in by Emily Miller. The car seat had kept Bluey from flying through the front window, but it was several hours before she, and her parents' bodies, were found on the rural Hinterland road by a passerby.

The realisation that Bluey had literally asked Emily to be her mother felt like a profound blessing. They'd always had such a good relationship, even through the dreaded rebellious teenage years, and now she could see why: *she had chosen Emily*. But adoption was supposed to be the other way around: a parent's choice!

Bluey looked at the heavy tome of her mother's deepest thoughts and feelings, lying on her lap. So private, so personal. This was a doorway into someone else's heart. This diary could take weeks, even months, to read. She wanted to absorb it all now, tonight, to feel her mother with her, but she also had to digest this new information. She had to put it into a context of the life she knew; or thought she knew.

Bluey fell asleep in Emily's bed, crying from exhaustion,

and slept fitfully till the raucous crows and their crazy aviary of an orchestra stirred her from slumber at five. There'd be no question of breakfast until she'd read some more.

Dear diary...
A little blonde angel came home with me today. I can't believe how in love I am with her. It's like we've always known each other. She's just so comfortable with me, as I am with her. The orphanage staff warned me that it would take months, maybe even years, for us to bond, and for her to form an attachment to me. How wrong they were! This little cherub called me Mummy from the second we were properly introduced, much to the chagrin of the staff, who were still deliberating on whether I'd be a suitable mother figure.

Three weeks later...
The records state her name is Maria Anastasia Herring, born October 23rd, but she won't answer to Maria. She keeps holding up her little blue blanket and saying 'Bluey'.

More for my own amusement, one day I called out 'Bluey, come and get some lunch', and she scampered into the kitchen. And from that day on I've only called her Bluey!

I have rearranged my work schedule so that I can be a full-time stay-at-home mother for Bluey. She goes to bed at 6pm, and my other work begins. There are plenty of orders for my dresses, and I sew like a mad woman till midnight each day. Bluey, bright as a button, is up at five. Bright as the sunshine. I'm exhausted, *but I wouldn't change this for the world. That little girl is everything to me. I never thought much about becoming a mother before I met her. It just wasn't something that was showing up on my radar. Bluey walked into my life, and into my heart. She tore me apart in the most beautiful way possible.*

Bluey said the words out loud: *she tore me apart in the most beautiful way possible.* Bluey's heart was now the one being torn apart. Why hadn't her mother ever shown her this before? It was such a beautiful exploration of their early days together, and she'd have loved nothing more than to have shared this.

Her fingers slowly traced the purple squares on her mother's patchwork quilt. Each patch, sewn by hand, from various left-over pieces of fabric from years of working as a seamstress. Emily Miller had loved the sensuality of fabric against the skin, and how you could transform a person, piece of furniture or a room with just the right colour, pattern and texture. She saw herself as an artist, and on every day of the week, whether she was in town or at home, Emily Miller took great care with how she dressed. Bluey smiled as she remembered the teenage years, and her black-clothes-only phase, and how often her mother grimaced as Bluey sauntered out the front door to meet up with her mates. It only lasted three months, but it tested Emily Miller's aesthetics to the limit.

Tuesday

Tuesday was spent reading more of the diary, and writing her eulogy for the funeral. Nadia had called Emily's friends, leaving Bluey to grieve in peace and save her energy for the farewell ceremony. Olivia popped by to offer moral support, and promised to be at the creekside well before the funeral tomorrow, and to help Nadia get the reception area ready. Dozens of bouquets were delivered to her door: thoughtful messages, blossoms of beauty. Baskets of fruit, and casseroles were left on the verandah. *Ice to the Eskimo,* she thought more than once as she popped another Tupperware container into her freezer. For once in her life, food was the farthest thing from her mind.

Dear diary...
We were standing in the supermarket aisle today, deciding on which lettuces to buy, when Bluey and I overheard two women gossiping nearby. They were saying that Bluey wasn't really my child. That she was adopted. I can't believe they'd say that in hearing distance of either me or Bluey!

Bluey marched right on over to them, her little blonde plaits flicking over her shoulders, storm cloud on her face, and hands on her three-year-old hips. 'Of course she's my Mummy! Silly!' I have never seen such a powerful person in my life. Those women ducked their heads and took off quick smart. Bluey skipped back over to me as if nothing had happened. Her face was bright like the Sun, and she simply said 'Get the baby lettuces, Mummy.' And then she kept giggling. The little minx!

At lunchtime, she stood on a chair by the kitchen sink washing the lettuces, tomatoes and cucumber as we prepared our meal. Bluey stopped what she was doing, and then said 'Do you know I love you Mummy?' She was so deadly serious. It really mattered to her that I knew. How could such a little girl be so thoughtful and aware? I've known people in their sixties who don't have as much wisdom as this little girl. I only hope that in her lifetime a lot of people get to meet her, and to share in the joy that I am so blessed to have.

Bluey laughed out loud. That was so her! She was more than capable of putting people in their place, and then continuing with whatever she was doing like nothing had happened. It wasn't that she didn't care about people; far from it. But she wasn't one to be walked over, either. She lost count of the times that people were taken in by her innocent face, and then tripped over themselves when the inner lioness began to roar.

She also thought of her job in the café. Sure it was always filled with the locals of Calico Bay, but there were plenty of tourists, too. She'd spent her adult life meeting all sorts of people, and she smiled at her mother's wish that she should meet many people throughout her life.

My Mother

Bluey sat up deep into the night, writing down her thoughts about life with Emily. How do you share such a profound and intimate relationship with others? How do you express a love so deep it carries on beyond death? Bluey was sharing a lifetime of precious moments and she wanted to get it just right. There'd only be one funeral. Only one chance to say goodbye properly. And Bluey wanted it to be beautiful, just like her mother.

Racing to her mother's blanket box with a sense of urgency, she opened it, her mind desperate to find what had led her there. Inside it was filled to the top with Winter bedding, but there, about half way down, she spied it: the object of her late-night memories. It was Bluey's little blue blanket. Holding it to her face, she slowly breathed in the scent of childhood. The scent she associated with Emily. Could she ever love another human the way that she loved her mother? She laughed to think of how Emily had kept hold of that blanket. So many times she wanted to wash the grubby little thing, but Bluey wouldn't let it out of her sight. At night time, she'd take it hostage by tying it in a knot around her arm so that Emily couldn't take it away. There was only one place for that blanket to be, and that was with Emily. Tomorrow, Bluey would place it in the coffin, alongside her beloved mother. They were the two constants in her childhood, and now it was time to let them both be free. Time for Bluey to stand on her own two feet.

It was 3am before Bluey felt satisfied with the eulogy. She wrote about finding the diary, and the impact of reading Emily's thoughts, and about standing at the orphanage gates.

Psychic Serena

One year earlier, Bluey had sought out a psychic to take up residency at the café each Saturday morning. She knew it would be a hit with the tourists.

Psychic Serena insisted she couldn't start unless she did a free reading for Olivia and Bluey. They both laughed it off, but eventually agreed.

Olivia heard promises of pregnancy, an overseas holiday and a windfall. She was sceptical, but hung onto the messages nevertheless.

Sitting in the private, velvet-curtained booth that was set up in a corner of the café, Serena warned Bluey of dark days to come. 'I don't say this to scare you, but to give you time. Plenty of time… There will be a lot of challenges, but you mustn't let them defeat you. You need to stay strong. Look, this tarot card is of death. Death isn't always a physical death, but a transformation. In fact, the transformation around you is so huge that I can't really predict what's on the other side. Some things aren't set in stone. We have choice; always a choice. You're going to be called on to make a lot of choices, and you need to find your inner power. You're going to come out of this time a different woman; stronger, more resilient, sure of yourself,' Serena promised her, sitting there in her pseudo-gypsy clothing: red headscarf tied around her silky black hair; and jangly silver earrings.

'It won't feel like it at the time, but you'll look back a few years from now and marvel at the changes that have happened within you. Oh, and one more thing: the man with dark hair and brown eyes? You can trust him. You'll recognise him by his kind hands.'

Bluey wasn't at all sure what to make of the reading, and she had no idea who the man with the dark hair was. She scoured her brain to think of every man in Calico Bay. Perhaps it was all a load of nonsense, but she hired Serena anyway. She also agreed to let her run a weekly astrology class on Tuesday afternoons. Bluey's ears always pricked up whenever Serena talked about the Sun sign of Scorpio: Bluey's zodiac sign.

Saturdays were always the busiest days in the café, and Serena never had a spare minute to herself. She took bookings all day long, and the faces that left her booth varied from delighted to perplexed to outraged. Most often though, it wasn't just the future she predicted, but the offering of a gentle ear to people's woes.

A Home Amongst the Gum Trees

Bluey was shocked by how many cars were parked on the beachside road in front of the café. It took her a few moments to realise they were all there for the funeral. Her mother was well known around Calico Bay, and further afield in Rallervale, but boy oh boy…she was not expecting this turnout.

Debating whether to go to the funeral home and travel with the body or to go straight to the site, she opted for parking her scooter at the back of the café, and began walking up towards Bendigo Creek.

'Bluey,' Olivia called out. 'I was just coming to find you. Are you okay?'

'As okay as I can ever be…' she replied, mournfully.

'Nadia's done a great job. It looks really beautiful. I can't believe how many people are here. I know your mother knew a lot of people, but Bluey, many of the mourners are here because they know *you*. It's really touching. There can't be anyone in Calico Bay who isn't here,' Olivia said. 'People really care for you, Bluey,' she offered kindly, taking her best friend by the hand. 'Come on, let's go up there.'

If Bluey thought there were a lot of cars, she was even more surprised by the number of people waiting up under the canopy of eucalyptus trees.

The day was cloaked in sweltering heat, and she was grateful for choosing not to wear funereal black. Instead, she opted for a light cotton, ankle-length ivory dress with gum-tree-green embroidery at the hemline. Her long blonde hair was tied up in a loose bun, with tendrils hanging freely around her cheekbones. She sighed deeply. There wasn't a face she didn't recognise.

All around this amphitheatre of her mother's farewell, were the faces of her life: from her childhood, and the life she'd carved as an adult. How could she not be moved?

People had taken time from their jobs to be here for her; to stand by her side and say 'we care'. Tears fell like raindrops from pewter clouds. Olivia squeezed her hand.

Nadia gathered everyone closer, and the sounds of Josie Staten's guitar sounded throughout the trees and across the creek. Josie had written a song that told of a mother and daughter love so deep it was a mirror of joy to all who witnessed them.

There wasn't a dry eye under those gum trees. The kookaburras stopped laughing out of respect for the occasion. For a few moments, anyway.

As Bluey listened, she felt the love of her community, and she knew, just knew, that she was going to be alright. It would be hard, painful even, but she could do this. She was a woman now, and not a little orphan girl standing at the gates waiting to be rescued. She was a woman. *A strong woman.*

Bluey felt droplets of sweat dripping from her forehead, despite the shade of the trees. She surveyed the tables which had been carried up, and the linen marquee over the reception area. Native Australian flowers filled huge vases and brought colour to the brown, green and grey bushland around her. Emily Miller had been right: this was the only place for her to be buried. Here, amongst the gum trees. This was always her home, and this was where she should take her final rest.

Nadia read out many of the tributes from Emily's friends, and spoke of her lifelong friendship with the woman who was known around the bay as The Sewing Lady. Bluey learnt that her mother didn't just sew clothes, but helped to sew people's lives together. There were countless stories of marriages repaired, and teenage cold wars that were stitched back together by her ability to listen and mediate. Bluey thought about the diary, and how there was so much about her mother that she didn't know, and today was echoing that. How come her mother hadn't shared all these stories? This was something to be proud of! That people came to Emily to help them repair and mend their lives appeared to be common knowledge to everyone but Bluey. She wondered how she'd missed it. Had she been too self-absorbed? Olivia would later remind her that all those acts of kindness had been administered in the spirit of confidentiality. There'd never been a need for Emily Miller to advertise her listening services.

Nadia invited Bluey to come and speak. She hesitated, and wondered if there was actually anything she could add to the ceremony. It appeared that Calico Bay knew Emily as well as she did, if not better. She took off her sandals, and walked across the red soil to where Nadia was standing by a small altar. Covered in a white cloth, it had protea flowers, a candle inside a glass jar, and a framed photo of Emily. The frame was handmade from myrtle wood by Pen Grille.

'As I stand here today, I feel there's nothing new that I can add to the story of Emily Miller. It seems you all knew her so well, and in fact, there are so many things I've learnt about her today that I wonder how well I actually knew her,' she said with an ironic smile. 'She was my best friend. Emily was my everything.' Bluey looked over to Mrs Saigest and Ms Harrington and said, 'When I was three years old, my mother and I overheard you in the supermarket saying that I wasn't really Emily's daughter. Apparently I put you in your place,' she smiled. The congregation laughed out loud. 'And I'll say the same thing today. She was the only mother I ever knew, and she was everything to me. Emily Miller couldn't have loved me more if I'd clambered out of her vagina.' Hoots of embarrassed laughter darted across the scrubland floor. Bluey smiled inwardly to see the reaction on some of the faces when she'd said the V word out loud. 'You see, being a mother isn't just about giving birth; it's about loving that person as much as you love yourself, if not more. Emily Miller loved me with all her soul.'

The congregation broke into spontaneous applause.

'She stitched your clothes, and she mended your marriages, and brought your wayward teenagers back home; but for me, she sewed my whole life into shape.' Bluey sighed, and then continued: 'I doubt there's another family in the world which could have given me more than my mother did.' Bluey acknowledged the life and love of Emily Miller with immense gratitude.

'I don't know if I'll ever be a mother; as you know, I haven't had the best of luck in the dating world, and marriage hasn't exactly been on the tarot cards, has it Serena?' She winked at her resident psychic. There was laughter all around. 'But if I was only half as loving, patient, kind and encouraging as Mum was, then I know I'll be a fantastic mother.'

Bluey paused for a few moments, allowing herself to get her breathing back into a gentle rhythm.

'I can't begin to express,' and she started crying softly, 'just how much it means to see you all here. To be honest, I thought it would just be me, Olivia, Pen Grille and a kangaroo here today! But look at you all! This is Calico Bay. This is my home. My life.'

She stopped for a moment to honour the tears slipping freely from her eyes. 'And…you're all part of that. I know I'm probably too old to need my mother, but I still do. I always will. I hope you realise you've all got very big shoes to fill!' She laughed as the tears cascaded down to her jawline, and then, one by one, dripped onto her dress.

Bluey pulled the blue blanket out of her bag. 'So many of you have wondered how I got to be called Bluey. Although it's common for Aussies with red hair to be nicknamed Blue or Bluey, obviously I haven't got red hair. I got my name for a different reason. Let me tell you…' she smiled, as she recalled the story in her mother's diary.

'On the day I chose Emily Miller to be my mother —yes, I chose her!—I was holding onto this little blue blanket inside the Oak Lane Orphanage gates. She could never get me to answer to my birth name, Maria, and one day, for a joke, she called me Bluey, as that was what I always called this blanket.'

The crowd of people around her laughed gently as they imagined a three-year-old version of the woman before them.

'Apparently I came running along as if it was the most natural thing in the world to go by that name. She never called me anything else after that. This blanket and Emily Miller were my childhood, and today, I'm saying goodbye to both of them.' She wept, knowing that the idea of putting it in with her mother was a lot easier than the reality. She softly stepped over to the willow coffin, which had been beautifully adorned with native wildflowers woven through the willow, and placed the blanket inside. Taking one long last look at her mother, she whispered 'Goodbye, Mum.'

Bluey stepped away, and moved to the loving embrace of Olivia, who held her for the longest time.

Nadia invited everyone to join her in prayer, and Pen Grille led five men from Calico Bay to gently lower the coffin into the earth. This was it now. Emily was not coming back.

Josie started strumming the guitar, and many people joined her in singing The Way We Were.

Can it be that it was all so simple then?
Or has time rewritten every line?
If we had the chance to do it all again
Tell me, would we? Could we?

It was some time before Bluey and Olivia joined everyone under the marquee.

'That was such a beautiful ceremony, Bluey. Really beautiful,' Olivia said encouragingly. 'So many funerals are almost anonymous. But this one was different. This was really about your mum. And that's so special. This is the time now to listen to more stories about her from all those people over there. This is the time when people are most open, and you'll hear stories you might never get the chance to hear again. Let this fill you up. Let them warm your heart. You'll carry them forever,' she said, so wisely. Bluey knew Olivia was right. Her father had died a few years before, and back then it was Bluey holding her hand; telling her to absorb everyone's memories.

Bluey was surprised by how pleasant the reception was and how light the mood appeared to be. There was love for Emily by the barrel-full, right alongside the platters of watermelon, papaya, mango mousse, and assorted foods on the buffet: falafel and baby pitta bread; stuffed vine leaves; tandoori tofu bites; mini asparagus tarts. A banquet of love. *Why did it take my mother's death to show me how valued I am in this community?* she wondered.

Nadia came up to Bluey and said she'd see to tidying everything up, and not to give it a thought.

'By the way, your mother didn't want a headstone, but it might be nice to plant something on the site so you can identify exactly which tree she's under,' she smiled gently, taking Bluey's hand. 'Sometimes they can all start looking the same!'

Bluey shook her head affirmatively, but couldn't speak at that moment. Nadia had handled every detail of the day; a true labour of love. She would miss Emily Miller just as much as Bluey.

'Make sure you take some time off before going back to work, okay? I can always come in and help Olivia if she likes, but you just take some time for you,' Nadia said in a motherly way.

'Yes, I will. I promise.'

Time Out

Bluey spent the next week not even thinking about the café, but sitting in the garden with home-made lemonade, or jogging on the beach. Other days she spent sorting through her mother's belongings, and sleeping. She'd never slept so much in her life. But grief had taken its toll, and she needed a sense of natural anaesthetic for her pain. She found it perfectly natural to sleep in Emily's bed, as it brought back countless memories of snuggling up there with her in childhood. There were times when she swore that she felt Emily's arms around her, or smelt her. And sometimes, she turned around to the sound of her name being called.

Dear diary...
I had a phone call from Maria Herring today.
It certainly took me by surprise. She made it
perfectly clear that she didn't want to raise
Bluey, but just wanted me to know that she
fully supported me in the adoption of her
granddaughter.

'Granddaughter? *Granddaughter?* Maria Herring?' Bluey said out loud. As far as she knew, she didn't have a grandmother: adopted or biological. Or did she? She continued reading, her heart thumping in her chest.

We agreed to meet up while Bluey was on a play
date with Olivia. I was so nervous. How could I
know for certain that she didn't want to take
away my daughter? MY DAUGHTER!

But she was ever so lovely. I quickly regretted
every single one of my possessive thoughts. Her
husband is dying of Parkinson's Disease, and she's

realistic enough to know that she can't raise a child as energetic and lively as Bluey, and nurse her husband through illness at the same time. I was saddened to see how grief stricken she still is over the death of her daughter.

Marlene was her only child, and little Maria (Bluey!) was the love of both their lives. I just can't believe that Bluey's never mentioned her, as she saw her most days when her mother was alive. Come to think of it, Bluey never mentions her birth mother. It's almost like that part of life didn't exist. I don't understand this. She's such a bright girl, who doesn't miss a trick. I mean, you couldn't fool her if you tried. And I have tried more than a few times! How come she doesn't ever mention her mother or grandmother?

Anyway, Maria Herring and I had a lovely afternoon together. I asked why Bluey's dad's family never took her in. Apparently, John and Marlene had never married, and his staunchly Catholic family took exception to this and didn't consider the child "viable" in their eyes. She was not a child of God! It took my breath away to hear this, and even more so when Maria went to great lengths to say what an incredible man he was. John had been a pilot for QANTAS and was working hard so that he and Marlene could buy some land in the countryside to raise their child.

Marlene was a retired stewardess, but before that had flown to just about every major city in the world. Theirs had been a love-at-first-sight romance, and they soon decided to start a family. They didn't want to wait. Little Maria was the light of their lives.

On the day they died, they were taking Maria to see the piece of land they were considering buying. They never made it there. A truck lost control as it turned a bend, and their dreams died right there on the roadside, melting into the hot bitumen.

Bluey stayed with Maria for a week, and was then placed in the orphanage. Maria said she cried solidly for a month after that, but she really felt it was the best option.

Maria insisted that I was Bluey's mother now, and she wanted to honour that. She felt it was best if she stayed out of her life, even though the thought of it was breaking her heart into a million pieces. But she did make me promise to send her photos and letters about Bluey, so that she could share in her life that way. I promised.

Bluey howled for an hour or more. She'd just lost her mother, but by reading this darn diary she'd now lost her *other* mother all over again. And her grandmother! Who was this Maria Herring? And how odd that there was another woman with the same name as her? Not that she ever thought of herself as Maria Herring! She was Bluey Miller, and as far as she was concerned, always had been. When the crying subsided, Bluey smiled to think she was born to parents who were so in love with each other. And then a thought crossed her mind: was Maria Herring still alive?

Pear and Chocolate Crumble

Home alone on Saturday night, instead of crawling into bed or watching late-night TV, Bluey headed to the kitchen. A small hessian sackful of ripe pears were begging for her to take notice of them. She peeled half a dozen, and sliced their tender juicy flesh in half, laying them in a pan with coconut oil and brown sugar. They began simmering. Their buttery and gritty flesh was perfect for a crumble. Coconut cream swirled around the pears, and a sprinkling of ground ginger dusted the top.

Bluey loved cooking with coconut, and always found it lent an erotic edge to her recipes, not to mention that it reminded her of Cole Hadden, a dashing young English businessmen who had taken her to dinner while in Jamaica several years ago. His kisses tasted like coconut with a hint of cinnamon and Caribbean sunshine. She could never look at coconuts in the same way again.

In another bowl, her hands mixed together flour, coconut oil, oats, raw brown sugar, desiccated coconut and two bars of dark ginger chocolate, broken into pieces. Bluey poured the creamy pear mixture into a casserole dish, and spread the crumble mixture on top, and then left it in the oven to bake for half an hour.

She peeked through the glass oven door, feeling a sense of satisfaction as the chocolate began to melt.

Whoever said that Eve left the garden of Eden for chocolate, was absolutely spot on!

What was the sudden craving for chocolate all about? She laughed when she realised her period was due any day. 'Ha, I need my boost of magnesium,' she said out loud. But thoughts of her body cycle only made her think of what it really meant: she wasn't pregnant, which was inevitable, as she wasn't having sex, which also meant she wasn't in a relationship or seeing anyone of significance. Why she'd think that when all thoughts should have been on her mother, she didn't know. She was startled at her train of procreative thoughts, and wondered what it must have been like for her mother to never have had a biological child.

Maria Herring

It was the day before she was due to go back to work, and a storm had brewed up on the horizon. Lead clouds hung low, like the apocalypse rushing forward to trample the world. Lightning zapped the bay, illuminating the sandy beach every few seconds. Bluey knew she shouldn't ride her scooter in this weather, but she couldn't help herself. She tried to ignore her mother's voice in her head. Putting on some rain gear over her jeans and purple hoodie, she headed up the motorway until she reached the town she was looking for. Jacaranda trees lined the road where Bluey stopped, and the old Queenslander boasted a freshly painted verandah. Bluey raced up the steps and took shelter, catching her breath before ringing the doorbell. It was at least a minute before the yellow door opened. There was no need for introductions. The old woman immediately recognised her granddaughter, and wept tears of joy. 'Come in my darling. Come in.'

Maria directed her to the lounge, and they sat on the brown corduroy sofa. 'Let me look at you,' she said, taking in almost thirty years of granddaughterly absence. 'Oh how I've missed you.' She shook her head, as if it had been the biggest regret of her life. 'I do hope you can forgive me,' she pleaded.

'Of course I do! What choice did you have? Really? I probably would have done the same. But, I'm here now.' Tears fell all over the place, with complete disregard for etiquette.

'Why now, my dear? Your mother promised me... Why did she tell you now?' Maria Herring asked.

'Mum died last week.' And with that Bluey was back to square one on the road of grief, trudging through the treacle of torment that comes with the painful loss of someone you love.

'I wondered why I hadn't heard anything from her for

a while. Come here my darling. Come here, hush now…'
And the arms of a loving grandmother were wrapped firmly around her fragile body. They both cried for some time. There were tears for love, for loss, for life, and now there were tears for reconciliation.

'Grandmother, I've never told anyone this, but…I never forgot you. I just…I just didn't *talk* about you. I could never forget the week you looked after me when Mum and Dad died. You held me all day long, and we sat in your rocking chair. You cried, you sang to me, you loved me. Maybe you were getting all your grandmothering into that one week, but I never forgot,' Bluey confided. 'I'd just forgotten that it was real. Really real. For all my life, I thought it was a good dream; the sort that can be hard to hang on to. I would go to that place in my heart quite often, especially when I was bullied at school. I'd just remember being rocked by you, and then I'd start smiling.' And with that, Bluey's face lit up for the first time in weeks, and her grandmother was blessed with that dose of sunshine that Emily Miller had enjoyed for twenty-six years.

'It's not too late, is it? Can we continue from here? Can I be your grandmother? I have no other family,' she said.

'Nor do I!' Bluey blubbed into her tissue. 'Nor do I…And no, it's never too late. You've always been my grandmother.'

'Dear, I'm so sorry about your mother. *Both* of your mothers!' she said, correcting herself.

'I know you are. Thank you.' Bluey looked at her watch. 'I need to go now, I've got an early start at work in the morning. Would you like to come to my place sometime? I can come and get you.'

'I would love that. Here's my phone number,' she said, scribbling it onto a piece of card. They hugged for the longest time. 'I wish you could have known how much love Marlene and John had for you. It was truly a love story, my dear.'

Bluey sniffed her way out of the door and back into the tears of the storm. 'Goodbye grandmother, I'll see you soon, yeah?' she asked.

'Yes, my dear', she said, busily wiping her own tears.

Chalkboard Menu

Bluey was up with the birds, and ready to start in the café early. It wasn't as if she'd suddenly stopped grieving, but today she felt the sort of lightness that comes after a storm has cleared the air. There was a distinct bounce in her step, and she thought she recognised her old Bluey self: the one who was there before her mother was diagnosed with leukaemia. Singing her favourite song, she plucked a few mangos from the tree in her front garden, and knew exactly what she'd do with them when she arrived at the café.

She popped the lush ripe fruits into her bag, placed them in the basket on the front of her scooter, and rode off into the rising light of dawn. It was a new day, and she felt fabulous for the first time in what seemed a very long time. She'd lived a lifetime in the past half year.

Bluey parked the scooter at the back of the café, and breathed in the fresh scent of morning air. The vegetables in the café garden were thriving. Several raised beds built from old railway sleepers supplied a lot of the produce, especially the fresh leafy greens like mizuna, pac choi, rocket, baby chard and beet.

The eucalyptus trees always smelt amazing after a storm. The scent of the earth made her feel so rich, and so alive. Once inside the kitchen, she set to work peeling the mangos and mashing the nectar-filled flesh.

The fruit of the goddesses, she thought to herself, licking the juice as it dripped from her slender fingers down her forearms. Bluey declared them the sexiest fruit of all.

Cole Hadden had shown her the best way to eat mangos: the *only* way to eat mangos. Naked. He insisted it was a private recipe.

Today she was making mango and cardamom cupcakes. Mixing the spelt flour and other dry ingredients with the mango, she added some freshly ground cardamom seeds. *Mmm*, she sighed, as they shot their citrusy fragrance her way. Smells good, Bluey thought, and popped a few trays of cupcakes into the oven, and then went to write up her chalkboard menu.

Goan potato and spinach soup, and soda bread
Cauliflower biryani with naan bread
Chilli-bean stew with nachos and guacamole
Mango and cardamom cupcakes
Emily Miller's chocolate pudding

And those last words didn't make her cry, much to her surprise. She smiled as she dusted the chalk off her fingers. And then she laughed. Bluey Miller continued to giggle as she recalled how often, as a child, she used to want her mother's secret recipe, and how Emily refused to give it to her. How very kind of Emily Miller to write the recipe near the front of her diary! She'd written about it in there because Bluey had asked for it for breakfast every morning for a week.

"Bluey needs pudding, Mummy. She needs it for *breakfast!*"

Onions sizzling in the pan were spiced with the heady combination of turmeric, ginger, cayenne, coriander, and cumin powder. The cauliflower, broken into florets, was added to the pan with some tomato paste and water. She placed the lid on, and set to work peeling the potatoes for the soup. Once they were done, and chopped into cubes, they bubbled away with onions in coconut milk.

Olivia had made the chilli bean and maple syrup stew the night before, so there was little left to do.

The chocolate pudding could be made later. Bluey laughed again to think how darn easy that recipe had been all along! There was another hour till opening time, and she nearly jumped out of her skin to hear a knock on the front glass window.

An open-topped jeep was parked out front, and a tall man stood there, looking out across the bay. He was dressed in faded denim jeans and a loose, white muslin shirt. His forearms were very well tanned. If only he looked as good from the front as he did from the back, she found herself thinking. And then he turned around. *Well that's a sight for sore eyes*, Bluey Miller almost said out loud. She smiled when their eyes met. *I want that for breakfast!*, she thought as she took in his dark hair, eyes, and freshly shaven face. His weather-worn skin erupted in crow's feet around his eyes, a testament to a life of laughter. She couldn't help but notice his chiselled nose, and the softness of his dark pink lips. Her mind was taking off in all sorts of directions, and her eyes were at serious risk of diabetes from consuming all that eye-candy.

Bluey unlocked the door, and the man apologised for the interruption.

'I know you're not open yet, sorry to disturb you, but I'm wondering if you could give me some directions?' he asked.

'Sure, where are you looking for?' she asked, colour rising in her cheeks as she took in the full picture of handsomeness before her. Her blush was a dead giveaway as to exactly what her body was feeling and her mind was thinking.

'Sandler's Nature Reserve. I followed the directions they sent me, but there's been a road closure due to the storm and fallen trees, and I'm clueless as to how to get there.'

Bluey said, 'Well, you're pretty close actually. It joins onto Pen Grille's land just behind the café. If you take that road there,' she said, pointing to a dirt lane adjacent to Bluey's Café, 'and follow it for a couple of minutes, you'll get there. Will you be working at Sandler's?' she asked, wondering if she might see him again.

'No, not really. I'm a freelance forest warden. I specialise in mediating land sales to ensure owners know the full consequences of what they're giving up when they sell to big business. You know that Pen Grille's land is up for sale, right?'

'WHAT?!' she almost screeched, hands on her hips in defiance. 'No, I did not! He hasn't said a word.' Bluey was furious. How dare he not say anything to her? That land was holy ground, and not just because her mother was buried out the back next to it, but because it had been in his family for generations and was made partially available to the residents of Calico Bay. Locals were free to take walks through there. It was an unspoken Nature Reserve that led onto Sandler's land.

'Sorry to be the bearer of bad news, Miss.. it *is* Miss?' he smiled, looking at her bare ring finger, and wondering exactly what her relationship status was.

'Yes, it's Miss. Miss Miller. Bluey, actually. Bluey Miller.' But she was less interested in sharing her name than wringing Pen Grille's neck. *How dare he?* He promised he'd never sell!

'Well, Bluey, it seems that times are tough, and he feels he has no choice but to sell. I'm trying to negotiate for Sandler's Reserve to buy it so that Calico Bay can keep the integrity of its landscape and heritage, but a big conglomerate has got its paw prints all over it so they can turn it into a theme park, holiday housing and every other nightmare you could have for that piece of land,' he said with tenderness, knowing what such a development would do to the area.

Bluey sat down on the nearest chair, trying to catch her breath. Her mother was hardly in the ground, and now she was facing another nightmare.

Psychic Serena had predicted challenging times ahead, but this was ridiculous! How could she save her café? How could she save this beautiful environment from ecological disaster?

He sat down at the same table.

'I'm sorry, I haven't even asked your name,' Bluey

said, realising her social skills had evaporated in the morning sea air.

'Clayton Lansen.' He smiled in a way that almost made her forget she was fuming. 'Bluey, I may not live here, but even a blind man could see what Jackson-Briggs Incorporated would do to this area. I don't want this beautiful stretch of land bulldozed down any more than you do. I'm here to fight your corner,' he said with sincerity.

'Well, Mr Lansen, the least I can do is offer you a coffee. How do you like it?' she asked, and headed to the coffee grinder.

'Latte would be great,' he said, his dark-green eyes following her.

She returned a minute later with his coffee, with no thought of the other jobs which needed to be done before opening the café.

'What happens now? Where do we go from here? How do we stop this happening?' she asked, hoping that she could draw all the answers from him in one sitting.

'I'm going to meet Josh Anderson at Sandler's in about an hour from now, and then later this morning we've got a meeting with Pen Grille. The truth is we just don't have the money that Jackson-Briggs is offering. They've laid more than double the market price on the table. I have to be honest, Bluey, this is going to be a tough fight. But I promise you this,' he said, his strong tanned hands reaching over to hers, and gently placing a supportive hand on hers. 'I'm not a man who gives up easily.'

'Well, you're in good company. I'll tie myself to those trees if I have to!'

She stood up, took off her apron, and headed out the back to the kitchen. Clayton wondered if she'd deserted him, but Bluey arrived back a moment later with a lunch box containing some freshly baked cupcakes.

'Here, you better keep up your strength,' she said, passing him her early morning creation.

'Best be on my way,' he said reluctantly, looking her up and down so he could remember exactly what she looked like after he walked out the door. Memorising each detail, so that if he never saw her again, he could be sure that he'd never forget the sight of her, or how she smelled of frangipanis on a Summer's night.

'These look fantastic,' he said, opening the lid and taking a deep breath. 'And smell great! Thank you. I'll drop the lunch box off later,' he winked, and headed out the door. She watched him get into the jeep, and start to drive away. Clayton looked back, and waved. A huge grin spread across his face.

Bluey sat down again. Calico Bay didn't make men like Clayton Lansen! Where was he from?

She smiled at the thought that he'd be returning to drop off the lunch box. *Pretty crafty Miss Miller, if I do say so myself!*

Olivia arrived ten minutes later, and was horrified to hear of the potential loss of the land behind Bluey's Café. 'But that's sacred land. That belongs to Calico Bay. We've all grown up playing amongst those trees, and swimming buck naked in the creek. Most of us had our first kiss down there! Who hasn't got a lifetime of memories from that bushland? How could Pen do this?' she asked, feeling as exasperated as Bluey did about the situation.

'Sounds like he doesn't have much choice. I didn't know he was in financial trouble. I can't believe it. I can't believe Mum didn't say anything. He's been offered double market value. He'd be stupid not to take the money and run...but he would be accountable to a lot of angry Calico residents. There must be something we can do. Maybe I could sell the house, and just rent a flat? Maybe I could go into partnership with Sandler's Reserve?' she said, exploring the possibility out loud.

'One thing's for sure, we have to find a way to appeal to Pen's better nature. He better not come in here for tea today!' Olivia said.

At 3pm, Bluey closed the front doors. 'It sure feels good to be back here,' she told Olivia. 'I met my grandmother last night. My *biological* grandmother. It was amazing,' Bluey said, telling her friend all about their meeting.

'I've been wondering why you seemed so much brighter today, Bluey, despite all the land nonsense with Pen.'

'It was therapeutic, that's for sure.' Bluey acknowledged. 'I'll finish up here, you go home.'

'Okay, see you tomorrow,' Olivia said, swinging her handbag over her shoulders, and heading out the door. She was short, 5' 1", and had curly brown hair, which she usually wore under a headscarf. It was too unruly to wear out during café hours.

Bluey cleared up the kitchen, and then unpacked some books which had arrived earlier by courier. At one end of the café, she kept a small bookshop of personal-growth and New Age books, crystals and incense. Tourists always loved this; it was like icing on the cake of the good food and drinks at Bluey's Café.

A couple of old comfortable armchairs, made of magenta-coloured velvet, and a small oak coffee table, were positioned by the hand-crafted wooden bookshelves, encouraging diners to linger for longer.

'Can I come in?' Clayton's voice asked tentatively from the partially open front door.

'Ah, it's lunch-box man. You really ought to try coming by in opening hours,' she suggested, with a huge smile on her face, knowing her crimson blush would once again advertise her feelings.

'I'll definitely try that next time,' he laughed, savouring her flirtatious tone.

Next time? *Fabulous*, she thought. *Can't wait!*

'It's been a tough day, Bluey,' he sighed. 'Really tough. I'm afraid I have to be somewhere else right now. I can't stay. Are you around tomorrow night?' he asked. 'I could come by then and fill you in.'

'Sure. What time? We shut at 3pm!' she warned him.

'It wouldn't be till about 7pm. Shall I meet you here, or down on the bay?' Clayton asked, allowing room for negotiation.

'I do declare, this is starting to sound like a date Mr Lansen.' Bluey laughed, and marvelled at how her old self was beginning to come back. How was that even possible?

'It could be, if you like? How about down by that huge bluff rock over there? We could get some chips and have dinner?' he suggested, hoping she'd respond.

'Sounds good to me. I'll pick them up and meet you then.'

Moonlight Serenade

The next day flew by, and before Bluey knew it, she was dressed in a long purple wrap-around skirt, and matching singlet top. She shut the front door of her home, and rode the scooter down to the bay. On the front of the bike, she had a picnic basket with a blanket, plates, drinks and salad. Henny's Chip Shop served the best chips for a hundred kilometres, or so the locals said. She ordered a couple of portions, some pineapple rings, and potato scallops in batter.

At the foot of bluff rock, she laid out the blanket, and set down plates, Greek salad and a bunch of grapes. She kept the chips in their wrapping paper, and hoped Clayton wouldn't be late. If there was one thing Bluey detested, it was cold, soggy chips. Right on seven o'clock, his jeep rolled on by and pulled up at the front of the café. Wearing rolled-up faded denim jeans, and a white T-shirt which highlighted his dark tan and hair, he strolled down onto the sand, barefoot, carrying his guitar and a bottle of wine.

'Blimey, this is a date, isn't it?' Bluey laughed.

'Anything wrong with that, Miss Miller? Some time in your company will make this job a whole lot more enjoyable for me,' Clayton smiled. He sat down on the blanket, opened the wine and then rubbed his eyes. Bluey could tell he'd had a long and tiring day.

She opened the chips from their wrappings, and shared them out with a generous helping of salad, too: romaine lettuce, feta cheese, cherry tomatoes, mint leaves, cucumber, onion and Kalamata olives, seasoned with oregano, sea salt and olive oil.

'Mmmmm,' he said, savouring the best salad he'd ever eaten. 'Tell me everything you know about Pen Grille. I need to understand him. What makes him tick? How long has he lived in the bay? Anything you can tell me will help,' Clayton asked, sounding more like a private detective than a forest ranger. 'I need to get a handle on his psychological profile, so I know who I'm dealing with.'

'I've known Pen almost all of my life. He's a man of few words, though. Very few words!' she said wryly. 'The strong silent type with the emphasis on silent. But Pen Grille's a good man. It might not seem like it from where you stand, or where I stand for that matter, but he's been like an uncle to me. He must have his reasons for selling. I don't believe it can be just about money. He could easily sell off small parcels of land if he wanted some cash flow. There's no need to sell the whole lot.'

The Sun was in skyfall to the horizon, and a full Moon rose steadily above the shoreline.

'Is he married? Does he have family here? What brought him to Calico Bay?' Clayton asked, firing off questions at rapid speed.

With a chip in her mouth, and tomato sauce on her fingers, Bluey finished chewing and then said, 'He's never been married. Come to think of it, I don't think I've ever seen him with a woman, apart from my mum, that is; but they were just friends. Good friends. The best of friends. Pen was always fiercely protective of her whenever it looked like some man was close to asking her out…'

She stopped in mid-sentence, a tear in her eye.

'Are you okay, Bluey?' he asked tenderly, noticing the change of expression on her face.

'Yeah,' she said, sniffing away her tears. 'I'm fine.'

'People don't cry if they're fine. Do you want to talk about it?' he asked.

Collecting her emotions, and pacing her breathing, she continued: 'I buried my mum less than two weeks ago. It still feels raw. And thinking of Pen protecting her just set me off. I'm sorry.'

'Why would you be sorry? I wouldn't have dragged you here if I knew you were grieving. I'm the sorry one.'

'I'm actually really glad you asked me. I like you Clayton. That's pretty obvious, isn't it?'

'The feeling's mutual. Would you like me to take you home or do you want to stay on?' he asked kindly.

'I want to stay here…with you.'

He leant forward to wipe a tear off her cheek, and then kissed the same spot. 'I'm so sorry for your loss, Bluey. That's a tough call losing a loved one. Really tough. How come you're back at work so soon?' he asked.

'The café is a comfortable place for me. I took time off, but now I need to just be around my familiar daily routine. It's good for me. And my friend Olivia can take over at a moment's notice if I lose the plot.'

'Is your dad still alive?' Clayton asked, as he took another serving of salad.

'Short answer or long answer?'

'There's a long answer?' Clayton asked, confused by how much more you need to say than a simple yes or no. He plucked a grape and gently fed it to Bluey, leaving his fingers by her lip just long enough for her to get the message. She was under his spell.

They talked for hours beneath the moonlight, just them and the lulling sound of the waves lapping on the shore. He eventually grabbed a blanket from the jeep to wrap around their shoulders when it grew too cool for comfort, and they sat, side by side, chatting about their lives.

'I think you know just about everything there is to know about me, Clayton.'

He laughed and said, 'You're not trying to get out of a second date, are you?'

'I thought I might have scared you off with my stories,' she said.

'They've had the opposite effect.' He smiled at Bluey and said, 'I've had the best night of my life tonight. Thank you.'

'Yeah, me too.'

Clayton picked up his guitar, and strummed the old Nat King Cole song *When I Fall In Love*.

After he finished, Bluey asked 'Why didn't you become a singer? Why are you a forest ranger?'

'I love both, and to be honest, I did think about singing professionally for a while, but I didn't like the idea of being reliant on an audience in order to feel good about myself. I tend to be a bit of a loner, and quite like my own company,' he admitted. 'But your company is pretty good, too,' he smiled. 'I do a gig once a month at my mate's pub. That's more than enough.'

'Sing me another song,' Bluey begged, and made herself comfortable on the blanket. He happily obliged:

> *Crazy, I'm crazy for feeling so lonely,*
> *I'm crazy, crazy for feeling so blue…*

'You should sing in the café while you're up here. The locals would love it! We could arrange an evening candlelit supper or something. Please say yes!' she pleaded. 'How long will you be in the bay?' Bluey asked, feeling a heaviness descend on her.

The realisation that Clayton Lansen wasn't going to be staying here permanently hit her hard. How had she fallen so darn quickly?

'I'm here for a few days until we can get Pen Grille to see sense. I've got other work to get back to, but I've promised the guys at Sandler's Reserve that I'll persevere and do what I can to get the land.' He could sense that she was already missing him, and he felt the same.

'I only live a couple of hours from here. You know, we can still see each other. It'll just require a bit of work to make it happen.'

Bluey nodded. How ridiculous she felt. They'd only been together a few hours, and now she couldn't live without him? She certainly was crazy!

'I best get home,' she said reluctantly. 'Early start in

the morning. Will you come by for a coffee?' she asked, hoping he'd say yes.

'Wouldn't miss it for the world! I'll have breakfast there, too.'

They walked, hand in hand, up to the roadside. Carefully placing his guitar in the jeep, he waited until she'd put the picnic basket on the front of her scooter, before asking 'May I kiss you?' But Clayton found himself not waiting for a reply. He scooped Bluey up into his arms and kissed her, softly, slowly and tenderly.

'Just as well I didn't say no,' Bluey smiled. 'I'll see you in the morning. I'll be there from six, but we don't open till seven am!' She got onto her scooter, and secured her helmet. 'Good night.'

'See ya,' he waved, sighing deeply as he drove off to the bed and breakfast at the southern end of the bay.

Pen Grille

Bluey smiled all the way home, and she smiled non-stop while having a twenty-minute shower. She smiled while she slipped into her cotton nightie, and she smiled when she sat on her mother's bed and opened the diary. Clayton Lansen had put that huge smile on her face, and she hoped it would stay there. She tried hard not to think about the fact that he wouldn't be staying in Calico Bay.

Bluey was awake for hours, reading about her childhood and the misadventures she'd got up to. It wasn't just the scraped knees or rescued crows she brought home, but wayward friends and hard-done-by strangers in the street. As a child, Bluey had believed her mother could fix everyone up. And after a few hours of reading, she noticed a common name that kept coming up: *Pen Grille*. To Bluey, Pen had always been on the periphery of their lives. Right from the start he'd said that Bluey and her friends could play on his land near Bendigo Creek. He often brought bags of tropical fruits for her and her mother, and would come by and service the car or mow the lawn. Pen Grille was like the sky: always there. Something you took for granted.

Dear diary...
Pen kissed me tonight. He confessed that he'd been longing to kiss me since grade seven when we were caught by the teacher next to the kissing tree! Everyone used to scratch their initials into the bark of the white gum tree. I don't know if he had ever seen P.G. 4 E.M. and the love heart I spent two hours scrawling with my pocket knife. If only he'd known that I was madly in love with him back then. Perhaps our lives would have been so different. If only that man would talk, but trying to get any

conversation out of him is like trying to pull out a hen's tooth. He's always been so quiet!

But tonight, he was like a different man. "I have to talk to you Miss Miller, and it can't wait." He'd come around after Bluey was in bed, like he always did. We'd sit and have a cup of tea on the verandah. It used to drive me nuts that he'd come to visit and then wouldn't say anything, but he seemed to get something out of coming by so I never deterred him. Tonight, though, he stood up on the verandah, looking out across the garden, and asked "Will you marry me?"

I was completely taken by surprise. Marriage? Where did that come from? I was too dumbstruck to answer. I stood there like an idiot, and it was as if our roles were reversed. Suddenly he became the talker. "I've loved you for so long, Emily, and I don't want to wait any longer. Marry me, and together we'll raise little Bluey. I promise I'll be a good father to her, and a good husband to you."

I still couldn't speak. Looking back, I couldn't have been more cruel, but to be honest, I just didn't know what to say. Of course I love Pen Grille! But ...well, life is different now. I have Bluey to think of. Bluey's fond of Pen, but I just don't see him as the fatherly type. Maybe I'm wrong, but I just don't know if I can take that risk. Bluey's been through far too much in her little life for me to put my feelings ahead of hers. Far too much! But oh my, that kiss! Who'd have thought Pen Grille had it in him? I have never in my life been kissed like that, and I've kissed more than a few men in my time.

Bluey stopped reading. Who the heck had her mum been kissing? How had she never noticed all those men? How did she not notice the chemistry between Pen and her mum? Bluey went to the kitchen and had a glass of water. The realisation that her mother had put her ahead of herself in such a profound way shook her to the core, and she found herself crying all over again. She wondered about Clayton, and what difference this bit of information might make. Is this why Pen is selling the land? Has he finally given up waiting for Mum now that she's dead? It was too late to phone Olivia and share this; she'd have to tell her in the morning.

Choppy Waters

Morning brought torrential rain and high winds whipping the shoreline. Bluey took off her wet-weather gear and hung them out the back of the café on the clothes line, and then went to freshen herself up and dry her hair. Her thoughts were all over the place this morning, as wild and frisky and untamed as the wind. *Probably not many customers today,* she mused, taking in the view of the battered bay.

She set the oven timer for the batches of chocolate and stem ginger cupcakes, and turned on the coffee machine. *Knock, knock, knock* came the sound of Clayton's knuckles rasping against the pane of the wet window.

'Quick, come in,' she said as she unlocked the front door. 'What a wild day!'

'Hey, good morning,' Clayton smiled, bringing her into his arms. 'I missed you last night.'

Suddenly the bad weather appeared to scamper over the horizon like a mucky puppy being shooed away, and her heart welled up. 'I missed you too.' And she let him kiss her. But this kiss was very different to last night's one: this was urgent, needy and hungry. They were both desperate for each other, and the reality that it would be some hours before they could be together properly tugged at them both.

'What would you like for breakfast?' Bluey asked, reluctantly pulling away. 'I can make you…'

'Just you. That's all I need,' he sighed, pulling her back into his arms and breathing in the scent of her skin.

'Pineapple and nutmeg muffins,' she said between kisses, 'Mushroom pancakes…'

'Mmmm, both of those…' he whispered.

'Chargrilled tofu...'

'Ahaaa, mmmm, yes,' Clayton said, not wanting to take a break from kissing her.

'Coconut and maple porridge…' she moaned at the deep pleasure coursing through her body as he kissed her ear lobe.

'I…really…have…to get ready for work,' Bluey sighed.

Clayton stood up straight. 'Mushroom pancakes it is then. When can I see you again?'

'I finish at 3pm, but tend to hang around for half an hour just to tidy up and plan the next day's menu. I'm free from about four or so, I suppose. Clayton, there's something you should know,' she said with great seriousness.

'You've got a boyfriend?' he asked, wondering if he'd jumped the gun.

'Boyfriend? No!' she said, shaking her head, and shocked that he'd think she'd two-time someone. 'It's about Pen Grille.'

'Oh,' he said, sounding relieved.

'He had quite a thing for my mum, as it turns out. You see, she's left me this diary of her life…well, her life from the time I came into it, that is. And well, he wanted to marry her. She declined because of me. I…well, I wonder if he's spent all these years waiting, hoping beyond hope, and trusting…that at some point she'd change her mind. They truly loved each other, but she put me first. I don't understand why they didn't at least hook up when I became an adult. I think that now she's dead, he's finally realised that his dream of marrying her is over. I think he's selling the land because he has no reason to stay now. I think he's lost the will to live.'

'I see,' Clayton said solemnly, and sighed. 'When a man's heart is broken, it's a pretty tough job to fix it up. At least I know where he's coming from now. I'll tread carefully. You have my word on that,' he promised.

'Clayton, I would never have expected anything less from you,' she smiled, heading off to the kitchen to fetch him breakfast.

'Can I join you in here?' he asked.

'Sure, and while you're here, stir that pot of soup for me,' she ordered, passing him a wooden spoon.

Bluey looked over at him, admiring his profile and well-toned body, and then turned to the job at hand. She poured the pancake batter into the pan, and added some sliced mushrooms. 'I can't imagine what it must be like to live your whole life waiting for someone to be with you, like Pen has done, and then to just have it vanish under your eyes like that. It breaks my heart, and I'm so bloody furious that I had no idea how smitten they were with each other. How could I have been so blind? I always thought my mum and I shared everything. I mean, we were really close...but since she's died I've discovered so many things she didn't share with me.'

Clayton left the wooden spoon in the soup pan and reached over to Bluey. He held her cheeks in the palms of his hands.

'Everyone needs to keep some things private. It's an important part of being human. You mustn't think it means that she loved you any less.'

'I know,' Bluey sniffed. 'I know...it's just that it feels like there's this whole other side to her that I didn't know.'

'You say she left you a diary? Well, she's sharing it with you now. Your mum didn't have to do that. She could have destroyed it before she died, if she wanted. This was her final gift to you, and it obviously meant a lot to her to have written in it for so long, and in such detail. That's what you have to treasure, Bluey; not the free-range thoughts trying to convince you that something was missing in your relationship. You need to be at peace with how things were between you both.'

He was so kind and thoughtful, and she could tell he meant every word that he said.

'She was lucky to have you for a daughter. Real lucky.'

Bluey served him mushroom pancakes, and carried the plate out into the seating area. 'Enjoy,' she said, as she prepared him a latte.

'So, Pen Grille, to your knowledge, doesn't have any other family?'

'No. He was an only child, like my mum,' she said, feeling sad at the thought that he truly had no one now. 'God I feel rotten. He led the team of men who lowered my mother's coffin into the ground, and I've not even asked him what that was like! He hasn't been in here since that day. And now, knowing what I do, that must have been the hardest day of his life. I'm such an idiot!' Bluey cried.

'Bluey, your mother had just died. You were deep in your own feelings. You had enough on your plate without wondering how everyone else was feeling. Stop beating yourself up.'

'I need to go and see him. I need to let him know that I know,' Bluey said, feeling a sense of urgency.

'Okay, well I'm due there this morning. Let me test the waters again, and I'll make arrangements for us to both go over tonight, okay?'

'Sure.'

Clayton ate his pancakes, and drank his coffee.

'I can see why you wanted to come back to work so quickly. This place is great. A real home away from home. If I lived in Calico Bay, I'd be in here all the time,' he laughed.

'Some of our customers feel like they live here, too.'

She smiled, and then her thoughts turned to her impending visit to Pen's house.

'Okay, I best be on my way. I know Pen's seeing some of the bigwigs from Jackson-Briggs today, so I want to see him first and see what I can do. Shall I pick you up from here at 4pm?'

'Actually, can you pick me up from home?' she asked, and scribbled the directions onto a paper napkin. He kissed her softly, and whispered, 'I miss you already.'

She smiled, and nestled into his shoulders. If only the rest of life could feel this safe.

'I'll see you later, then,' Bluey said, breathing him in to her heart.

Olivia turned up half an hour later, and the first thing she said was 'Are you in love? You just look so darned happy!'

'Do I?' Bluey asked, somewhat startled by the question.

'You're confusing me. I know you're grieving, but I've never seen you look so good. What's going on?' she demanded, in a best-friend sort of way.

'Must be the weather!' she laughed, looking at the windswept trees, and rain crashing into the windows.

'Why did you make so much food, Bluey? In this weather, we probably won't get a single customer!' Olivia said, fussing at the amount of food already prepared.

'Don't worry about it...Some of it will freeze. Why don't you just enjoy the peace and quiet for a bit?' Bluey said, pulling up a chair and reading the local weekly newspaper: the Calico Bay Chronicle.

Olivia brought over a pot of peppermint tea, and pulled up a chair too. 'I should have stayed in bed,' she moaned, as the rain continued to batter the large windows. 'We haven't had weather like this for years.'

'Mmm,' Bluey agreed, head deep in the back of the paper, reading the dozens of tributes to her mother. 'Have you seen these?' she asked Olivia, passing over the paper.

'Yes, I have. They're beautiful, aren't they?'

They both looked up when two large vehicles with Jackson-Briggs written on the sides pulled up outside the café. Bluey's stomach turned inside out.

'They better not be coming in here!' she snapped.

'I don't think we can be too fussy on a day like today, can we?' Olivia said.

Eight men, dressed in business suits and phallic ties, scrambled beneath black umbrellas through the driving rain and gale-force winds.

'Ladies,' the first man acknowledged as he shook his head inside the front door.

'I'll get you some towels to dry yourselves off,' Bluey said, heading to the kitchen.

They all seated themselves around two tables, pushing them together to form one. *They already think they own the place*, Bluey said to herself as she gave them each a towel. 'Coffee?' she asked, but didn't show her usual smiley self to them. She wanted to kick them in the shins; the whole darn lot of them.

How dare they come driving up here to her little community, and plan to take it over with their corporate concrete constructions. Bluey was tempted to drop a coffee in one of their laps, but refrained. She could see Olivia out of the corner of her eye, waiting, just waiting for Bluey to put them in their place. Olivia was on edge: she knew Bluey far too well!

The men ordered meals from the chalkboard menu, and Bluey was grateful, in a roundabout way, that no food was going to waste.

'Be a shame for this little café to go,' Bluey heard the ginger-haired man say.

Over my bloody dead body, she muttered under her breath.

Olivia and Bluey listened breathlessly from the kitchen as plans for the land were discussed in great detail. Bluey's heart sank. How could Pen do this to her? To Calico Bay? People moved to the bay precisely because there was very little here. They loved the quiet life, and lack of chain shops. Bluey's Café was the only building on this stretch of road, with the other independent shops at the southern end of the bay. Jackson-Briggs would change the whole ecology of this area.

'I think we should rename it Jackson Bay, just so the locals are under no illusions,' the older, grey-haired man snickered, gathering more ruthless jibes and chuckles from his companions.

'I hope he chokes on his coffee,' Bluey whispered to Olivia, and was already mentally planning his demise.

'They make me so angry!'

The men stayed in Bluey's Café for two hours, driving the women to distraction with their snide comments about hick towns and independent shops. They left an embarrassingly large tip behind for Olivia and Bluey, and the women were in two minds about whether to keep it or donate it to charity.

They'd barely been gone for half an hour, when they returned and took up seats in the café.

'I know we're good, gentlemen, but I didn't realise we were that good!' Bluey said, astonished by their quick return.

'Change of plans. We had a business meeting, but the road's been blocked by an ambulance. We'll have to try again later.'

Bluey panicked. There weren't any other houses up Pen's road. Why would there be an ambulance there? 'Olivia, I have to go. I think Clayton's been hurt!' The words were hardly out of Bluey's mouth before she was out of the back door and on her scooter. She didn't even bother with her wet-weather gear.

The scooter was pushed to its limit, and despite the driving rain scratching her face, she sped up Pinara Road. But when she got there, the ambulance was gone. There was no sign of Clayton. Bluey started to cry. Pen's car was in the driveway, but there wasn't anyone around. She banged on his front door furiously. Bluey got back on her scooter and rode to the one place she hoped she'd never have to visit again: Holly End Hospital.

Parking the scooter in the staff car park because she didn't have coins on her for the parking meter, she raced into the Accident and Emergency area. She was shocked to see Clayton standing there, crying.

'Clayton? What is it? I thought you must have been hurt...' Bluey cried, falling into his arms.

'I'm fine. But, well, I'm sorry,' he said, pulling her

close and kissing her forehead. 'It's…Pen's dead, Bluey. I'm so sorry,' he said, hugging her tight.

'What?' she asked, hardly able to take in the news.

'He died on the way here. He suffered a heart attack at the house, but by the time we got here, Pen was gone. The damage was too severe.'

She sobbed deeply, not caring what anyone thought of her emotions. *No, no, no!* This hurt! Today she was going to talk to Pen about his love for her mother, and how sorry she was that she'd got in the way of that; and now she couldn't. She could never tell him.

'He was in such a state because he'd signed over the land to Jackson-Briggs last night, and was regretting it. I told Pen you knew about him and Emily, and he said the land was always meant to be for her. Pen said he'd lost the will to live and that Emily was the love of his life, and that they'd had an affair for many years. He stopped coming around at night when you refused to go to bed at a decent hour.' Clayton couldn't help an ironic smile at the thought of Bluey being an inhibitor to Pen's sexual advances towards her mother; then he remembered the gravity of where they were. 'And then, he just clutched his arm. I called the ambulance, but …'

Bluey sat on the concrete floor of the ambulance bay and cried. Eventually, Clayton lifted her up and carried her to his jeep. They sat there for an hour, in the pouring rain, soaked to the skin, not saying a word. 'I'll take you home now,' he said softly, and then lifted her scooter into the back of the jeep.

'Have you got a mobile phone on you, Clayton?' she asked.

He handed it to her, and she dialled the café. 'Olivia, get those bloody men out of there, and don't ever let them back in!' she yelled, the venom shocking Clayton back to reality.

'Sweetheart, I know you're angry, but they didn't kill him. Pen died of a broken heart.'

'Maybe, but I don't want them as my neighbours. You know they're going to force me to sell. They'll leave me no choice. My mother put everything she had into that place. I could never have bought the land and building on my own. You don't exactly make a fortune selling coffee and sandwiches.'

Clayton left Bluey to her thoughts, and followed her directions home. When they pulled up in the drive, Clayton told her that he was staying with her for the night. 'I'm not going anywhere, Bluey. I'll sleep on the sofa, but you need to know that I'm here.'

'Like hell you're sleeping on the sofa!' she huffed as she dragged him through the front door. 'Let's get out of these wet clothes,' she said, pulling off her skirt and top, and leaving them in a puddle on the polished wood floor. He followed her naked body, and left his clothes behind too. They stepped into the steaming shower, and held each other beneath the flow of hot water. He washed her back, kissed her, and held her as the tears fell, not knowing where they started and the shower began. Several minutes later, Clayton dried her off with a towel, and then himself. She led him to her bedroom. It would be the first time she'd slept in there since she started reading the diary. They spent the afternoon and evening talking to each other, then fell asleep in each other's arms, and didn't wake up until first light.

'Pen didn't have anyone. Who'll take care of his funeral arrangements?' Bluey asked Clayton, as soon as his eyes opened.

'I guess the local solicitor would probably have information on next of kin and things like that. That might be the best place to start. Bluey, my work here is finished. I've not succeeded, and I'm so desperately sorry. I'll stay here until after the funeral, but then we're going to have to work out the best way of seeing each other.' Clayton stroked her cheek, and wiped away the tears. 'Come on, let's head down to the town and see what we can find out. Will Olivia be able to take care of the café today?'

'Yeah, of course she will.' But Bluey's mind was elsewhere. When she thought of Pen Grille, she thought of her mother. They should have been together, and she—Bluey Miller—had got in the way of that. Now she was going to bring them together. 'I want him buried next to my mother, down by Bendigo Creek. He deserves that, at least. That land is my mother's land... well, I suppose it's mine now. I haven't even looked into the legality of that yet. Jackson-Briggs might be able to boot me out of the café, but they'll never touch that strip of land. Ever!' she said fiercely.

'Okay then, let's make it happen,' he said, assuring her.

Bluey dressed in denim shorts, cut from old faded and torn jeans, and a green floral blouse. She wore her long honey-blonde hair up high in a matching lime-green scrunchie.

They headed down to the bay, and into Hart Joiner and Sons, Solicitors.

Hart was the same age as Pen. They had been schoolboy friends. He broke down upon hearing the news.

'Pen was a man of few words, but by God he was a good man. I'm gonna miss that old codger.' He stifled his tears, and said 'Right, you're not here to see me cry. Yes, Pen's legal affairs are with me. I think you should know that he's already got a plot of land arranged for his burial. He sorted it out about six months ago. I don't want to upset you, Bluey, but you should know that he wanted to be buried alongside your mother. It was something they'd decided together when they realised she wasn't going to get any better.'

Bluey cried and laughed at the same time. 'I'm not upset! I couldn't be happier! Well, considering the circumstances. Hart, he's sold the land and his house to Jackson-Briggs. He signed off on them two days ago.'

'Yes, I know. I've got all the paperwork here to send off to Jackson-Briggs. I'm sorry, Bluey. I tried to talk him out of it, but he was adamant that he wanted to sell up and move a long way from here. He died a broken man,' Hart declared. 'I guess the diggers and construction teams will move in pretty quickly. Look, it's not up to me to give you unwanted legal advice, Bluey, but you don't have to sell. They can't make you. Your café's reputation is strong and solid. Sure the environment around it will change, but you can survive that. And you'll still have your mother's strip of land. It won't all be a concrete jungle. Just hang in there!' he encouraged her.

Clayton held Bluey's hand as she said 'Thanks so much for your help, Hart. We'll head down to the funeral home and make arrangements.'

They shook hands, and Clayton and Bluey walked down the street to Calico Bay Funeral Home. 'We should have the funeral reception at the café. Pen liked to come in for his pot of Earl Grey tea. I'm sure we could squeeze everyone in,' she said, wanting to give this man something in death that she hadn't done in life.

'Whatever you want, we'll make it happen,' Clayton promised her.

The staff at the funeral home were shocked and saddened that Bluey was having to walk down this road again, and gave her all the support they could. Bluey told Clayton that she needed to go to the café, and they walked the length of the bay rather than driving.

'Hey Olivia,' she said, and then took her out the back to fill her in on what had been happening.

'Bluey, I can't believe this,' Olivia said, shaking her head as she watched Bluey write a notice for the front door of the café.

We are honoured to hold the funeral reception of
Pen Grille here at Bluey's Café, on Saturday at 4pm,
following the ceremony at Bendigo Creek.

'We'll need to make plenty of food,' Bluey said,

slipping into efficiency mode.

'There's plenty of time for that,' Clayton insisted, and then grabbed her by the hand. 'Come with me.' He led her down to the beach. 'You really need to pace yourself. You're still in shock and grief from your mother's death. As much as you might like cooking, you need to just stand back for a bit and breathe. Olivia's got everything in hand. Let's go for a walk on the sand. You don't have to talk if you don't want to, but I'm here for you if you do,' he said, stroking her hand.

'Where did you come from? I can't believe you've arrived in my life at this time, like an angel. I don't know how I'd have got through this week without you,' she said, kissing him on the cheek.

They ambled along the beach, barefoot, for an hour, before turning back. It was late, and they were both hungry. Bluey opened the back door of the café, and they helped themselves to chickpea burgers with red capsicum and pineapple relish. 'Wow, Olivia did a great job with these!' Bluey said between bites. 'Yum. I didn't realise how famished I was.'

'Let's get you home to sleep. Come on,' Clayton said, after clearing the dishes.

What If?

They showered, and climbed into bed.

'Clayton, would you mind if I read some more of my mother's diary before we go to sleep. I didn't get to read yesterday, and I feel like there's something missing from my day,' Bluey said.

'Of course not,' he replied, and she headed to her mother's bedroom to bring it back to her own room.

'Would it be wrong if I read it out loud to you?' she asked.

'It's yours now, Bluey, not your mum's. She gave it to you. It's up to you what you do with it,' he said, encouraging her to follow her heart.

Dear diary...
I'm busier than ever with my sewing. Bluey needs more and more clothes. She's growing like a beanstalk. I can't keep up with her. There's always some thing or other she needs for school, too, and I'm grateful for the extra income.
She made me laugh so hard today when she tried to put on my three-inch high heels, and, in her words: 'beed a growned-up woman.'

There can't be a day goes by where she doesn't make me laugh. Her smile is infectious. I've often wondered how I lived for so long without her in my life. But right now I feel like I'm living a double life.

By day I'm a mother and a seamstress, and at night when she's tucked up in bed, Pen and I head out to the spare room to make love. He's so tender, and holds me like I'm the only woman in the world.

There's so much that goes on inside of him, but he doesn't express it in words. I swear someone cut out his tongue when he was a lad! I once said to him "Has the cat got your tongue?" and he looked like he had seen a ghost. When he makes love to me, though, I know exactly what he's thinking. I'm not sure if he's forgiven me for not marrying him, but he hasn't stopped coming by each night. If only life was less complicated.

Two months later...
The lady from the school office phoned and said "Please don't panic Miss Miller, but little Bluey's in hospital. Please don't worry, but we urge you to go down there as soon as possible." Did she really expect me not to panic?! I was hysterical before I'd even left the front door. I've never driven so fast in my life. Pen was already there. I phoned him as I left, and when I arrived he had his arms around Bluey, as she lay there whimpering, calling out for me.

She'd been pushed off the slippery slide by the Boydam boys (wait till I get my hands on their scruffy little necks!), and injured her foot. Pen and I sat with her for hours, bathed in the hospital stench of industrial-grade disinfectant, blinded by harsh fluorescent lights, and the clanging of hospital trolleys down the hallway. I hate hospitals, and hope I never have to step inside one again. Bluey had perked up pretty quickly once Pen had arrived, and was more than sedated with a bowl of jelly! That girl and food, they were made for each other. I bet she'll never make me a grandmother: she'll marry a bowl of pasta before she looks at what a man can offer her!

'I hope she's not right about the food,' Clayton laughed, imagining Bluey preferring a bowl of pasta to him.

She looked at him seriously, and then said 'I think I'd choose you over pasta.'

'You think?' he said, tickling her and making her laugh uncontrollably. When she stopped, he kissed her tenderly, deeply and passionately.

'Pasta can't do *that*!' she smiled, picking up the diary again.

I started bleeding tonight. I guess it was the shock of Bluey's accident. When they phoned to tell me she was in hospital, my mind immediately created the worst possible scenario. It scared the life out of me, literally. I swear I couldn't live without that girl by my side.

I don't think my body is going to hold onto this baby. I don't know how I'm going to let Pen know. He was so excited when I finally got around to telling him last week.

Bluey looked over to Clayton. 'I never knew she was pregnant. She never said anything, not even when I was an adult.'

He actually said more than five words when I shared the news of our pregnancy. "I'm going to be a father? We're having a baby!" he announced excitedly, in a way which was most uncharacteristic of him. He actually lifted me off the floor, and danced around the room with me. This is going to break his heart. I think Bluey would have been ready for a little brother or sister. She's settled in so well, and is so happy.

Three weeks later...
The baby has gone. Dr Baker confirmed it. Pen
hasn't said a word these past three weeks. He's
been here every night, but is deathly silent. I'm
sure I saw a tear in his eye last night when we
made love. People think that not much goes on
inside Pen, but I know otherwise.

He feels things so deeply that I think it just
becomes pointless to talk about them...as if words
make the experience or the feeling shallow,
somehow. But he's feeling this loss so painfully.
We'd never talked about having children
together. For me, Bluey has always been enough.
She always will be enough. That ray of sunshine
is my whole world. Pen's part of that, of course,
but Bluey's my little girl. She needs me. Though,
in fairness, this week I've discovered Pen needs
me too. I can feel it in the way he holds me, and
when he enters my body there's a sense of doing
everything he can to become one with me so
that we're so connected I'll never leave him.

Bluey put the book down, and let Clayton hold her for the
longest time. 'I can't believe I got in the way of their love
for each other. That just feels so wrong.'

'Don't start feeling guilty, Bluey. Life is nothing more
than a bunch of choices. Your mum could have chosen
differently, but she followed her heart.'

I find it impossible to explain to Pen—not that
he's ever asked me to explain it—that he's no less
important to me because we don't live together
or we're not married. Perhaps it's because our
relationship is so private, and no one knows
about it, that I feel guilty. I never intended on it
being a secret affair. All I was doing was trying

not to confuse Bluey by having a man come into the house all the time.

She sees Pen often enough, but as an "uncle" figure, not as my lover or as her father. It scares me how that little girl can read my mind, though. Today she said, "I'd quite like a sister. Can you get me one?"

She saw my expression change, and went off to play with her dolls. An hour later she came back and said "I can find a daddy if you like." That called for a glass of wine! I never drink, but in that moment I felt like there were no boundaries at all between us, and that we were so psychically connected that she must know about Pen.

"Pen could be the dad," she said matter of factly over breakfast the next day.

The Diggers

At six in the morning, Bluey was mopping the wooden floor of her café, with half an eye on watching the Sun rise over the red horizon. A glorious day. That is, until no less than ten diggers came driving by in quick succession. Her heart fell right down onto the floorboards. Oh no! She knew exactly where they were heading.

This couldn't be possible. The land deal might have been signed already, but Pen Grille wasn't even in the ground! It was wrong that his property should be dealt with like this. Jumping on her scooter, she raced around to Pen's house, using the back track by Bendigo Creek so she could head them off before they got in his front gate.

She stood, feet glued to the ground, hands on hips, and waited for them to arrive. Bluey was all ready to bite someone's head off, but the first driver there was quick to point out that they were only delivering the machinery. They weren't commencing for another week or so.

'Well, I don't see why any of you have to be here. That man's not even six feet under and you're ready to raze his land to the ground. It's disgusting. I swear, if anyone lays a finger on this land before his funeral, there'll be hell to pay. And don't you dare think that just because I'm a woman you can walk all over me....I'm a lot tougher than I look,' she spat. Bluey was in tears as she walked away from them, so she didn't hear the workmen snickering. She arrived back at the café to find Clayton finishing the mopping.

'Hey, I didn't expect you here for a while,' she said, wiping her tears. 'I thought you'd have a sleep-in after our late night.'

'Honey, what's the matter?' Clayton asked, holding her close.

'The diggers have arrived. They're ready to start removing the scrubland. I can't bear the thought of all those trees going. And Pen's house. They'll most certainly demolish that.'

'Sweetheart, I've taken a break from work so I can be here to help you go through his things, and sort everything out. You don't have to do this alone. I'm here for you,' he promised, soothing her brow.

'Why are you being so nice to me?' She blubbed into a tissue.

'Everything about you, Bluey Miller, makes me want to be nice to you. You bring out the best in me. Now, just let me help. Hart phoned while you were out. He said he'd drop off the keys to Pen's house later, and fill you in on whatever you need to know. So, what job can I do next?'

She nodded in acknowledgement and gratitude. 'Um, I'll just write up the menu and you can help me prep the food if you like. Olivia will be in at eight this morning,' she said, sighing, 'so I could really do with your help. I'm just not in the right head space to do this alone,' she said, breathing deeply to hold back the tears.

Spicy couscous and fennel, lime and coconut salad
Crispy artichoke nuggets
Beetroot and cumin tart
Lemon cake with frosting
Strawberry sorbet

'How do you not weigh twenty stone with all this food to eat every day?' Clayton asked, his mouth watering.

'I cook it, I don't eat it!' she laughed, grateful for the change in conversation. 'And if you look carefully, you'll see that it's usually pretty healthy food. Good-tasting food doesn't have to be bad for you,' she smiled.

Bluey soaked the couscous in boiling water, and added some sultanas and Moroccan spices. Clayton sliced the fennel, and grated the limes for zest. Three lemon cakes baked: the scent of fresh lemons infusing the air.

'I think we're almost done. Olivia made the beetroot tart last night, and the sorbet has been in the freezer for a few days. The batter for the artichoke nuggets is done, so… let's have a coffee. Shall we sit on the verandah? It's such an amazing morning, well, weather-wise at least,' she said, her mood lowering again at the thought of those men in their little Tonka trucks.

Just as they were finishing their coffee, the first customer arrived: it was Hart.

'Hey there, sorry to disturb your coffee, but I wanted to catch you before the rush,' he said. Hart took a seat, and sighed.

'Pen was a good mate of mine. He didn't say much, but one thing I know that probably no one else in this town does, is that you and your mum were everything to him. You were his family. I think that in your mum's absence, Bluey, he'd want you to step into her shoes.'

'I would be honoured, Hart,' was all she said. Bluey didn't feel like sharing what she'd read in the diary. She could tell that Hart had a pretty good idea of what went on between Pen Grille and Emily Miller for all those years.

'When can I start? The bloody diggers are already up there, you know!' she said, steam coming out of her ears.

Hart handed her the keys. 'Start as soon as you want. You know the house is going to be demolished?' he said sadly. 'It really was like Pen wanted to get rid of his life and start again.'

Hart looked over to the bay, then looked up at the café behind him. 'This is a perfect place to have the funeral reception. Pen wouldn't have wanted a fuss, you know, but people will want to pay their respects. He might have been a quiet man, but one thing is true: no one here had a bad word to say about him. He was like your mum in many ways. She mended people's hearts, and he mended their cars, and lawnmowers, and…'

'And my scooter, and my hot-water boiler,' she laughed. 'Yep, they were a pair of menders alright.'

Clayton squeezed her hand. 'Perhaps if it's not too busy this morning, we can head over when Olivia gets here?'

'Yeah, sure. Thanks for everything, Hart. Pen was lucky to have you for a friend.'

'No Bluey, I was the lucky one. Men like Pen are few and far between.' Hart said, standing up and waving goodbye. They could see he was too choked up to say anything else.

Farewell Old Fella

The burial of Pen Grille was simple: he was wrapped in a cloth shroud, as had been his wish, and buried next to the love of his life, Emily Miller. They were together now, forever. Bluey felt a sense of peace about this as she placed a bunch of native Australian flowers at the end of his resting place: banksias, various eucalyptus foliage, cones and gumnuts, protea, bottlebrush, Sturt desert pea, wattle and black grass. It was a fitting floral tribute to a man of the bush.

There hadn't been a hearse or funeral procession of black cars. The body of Pen Grille had been brought to Bendigo Creek on a horse and cart. Hart led the way, and spoke eloquently about the "man of few words".

'When Pen Grille spoke, you listened. If he had something to say, you knew it was damned-well important and you stopped everything to pay attention. We could all learn a lot from that. I'm going to miss him more than you could imagine. He was my best friend. Farewell Pen, Calico Bay will be less of a place without you, mate.' As Hart unapologetically dissolved into tears before the crowd of mourners, Bluey went up and hugged him. They were joined in grief.

After the ceremony, the mourners walked back to Bluey's Café. Bluey had burned rose incense, and filled the space with native flowers. Trays of food were brought out, and Olivia and friends walked amongst the people sharing food and drinks. There were falafel, and mini pitta breads, baby-artichoke tarts, dips and spreads and vegetable crudités.

Hart called for everyone's attention. 'Please raise your glasses to Pen Grille.' And that was all that needed to be said. Bluey and Clayton held hands for the afternoon, smiling at the stories which emerged from the locals about the quiet man.

At sunset, people left the café. Bluey lit some candles, and put on a Be Good Tanyas CD. Their plaintive and haunting voices, with lonesome harmonies, suited her mood perfectly.

'Dance with me, Clayton. Hold me close,' she said, with a sense of urgency. 'It's been a rough couple of weeks, to say the least. And there are more tough times to come as I watch Pen's life be bulldozed to the ground… and you're going to go home…and my heart is going to break into a million pieces. How did I let myself fall for you so deeply?'

Bluey's blonde hair draped her cheekbones, as she looked to the ground.

Clayton pulled her chin up, gently.

'Let's just focus on today, and then the next day. We don't need to worry about something that hasn't even happened yet, do we?' Clayton rubbed his eyes. 'I'm beat, and could do with a good night's sleep. We've still got to finish going through Pen's things before Jackson-Briggs starts in two days.'

Clayton held her close for a slow dance.

'I've fallen in love with you, Bluey Miller. I'm not going anywhere.'

Bluey wasn't sure if he'd actually said those words, or if she simply imagined them. By ten that night, they were in bed, asleep.

Bluey awoke a few hours later to Clayton's hand on her breast. She responded, and kissed him to say 'yes'. The next few hours of the still-dark night were some of the best Bluey had ever experienced. Clayton showed her, slowly and deliberately, what it meant to make love to a woman.

They explored each other with a depth of honesty and kindness that neither of them had experienced with another human. Lovemaking brought them to tears, and they held each other as one.

Bluey wanted to love him until she died, if not for longer. Skin to skin, breath to breath; their lips lingered over each other's body, slowly absorbing what the other enjoyed and responded to, and like dancers, they moved: one step forward, one step back. They waltzed to the sound of their own music, and in those dark and silent hours, they were the only people alive. The only noises of the night were the unmistakeable sounds of pleasure. It was pretty simple: they couldn't be apart again.

'I can't believe I waited so long to make love to you,' he whispered afterwards.

'Well, the timing hasn't exactly been right before now, has it?' she murmured while kissing his bare shoulder. 'It feels so good being with you. It's like you've always been in my life. I can't actually remember a time when you weren't around. That sounds so stupid, doesn't it?'

'No honey, it doesn't. I feel the same.' He kissed her again, and their bodies once again became one. By sunrise, they fell into a deep sleep.

At just after eight in the morning, the phone stunned them into the bleaching light of a new day.

'Hello,' Bluey answered groggily.

'Any plans of coming into work today?' Olivia asked down the phone line.

'What?' Bluey mumbled, looking at the bedside clock. 'Crap. I'll be there in half an hour!' She hung up the phone, and raced to the shower.

Clayton followed her in; holding her, washing her, kissing her into the day.

'How am I going to get to work if you keep doing that?' she asked.

'I just want to leave you in no doubt, Miss Miller, that you'll choose me over pasta any day of the week.'

'There's something you should know, Mr Lansen,' she teased as she took the soap and started to wash him, 'I don't actually like pasta!'

Her laughter was contagious, her giggles rippling

throughout the house, and he wrapped his arms around her and said, 'I love you so much!'

With a smile on her face, Bluey got into the passenger seat of Clayton's jeep, and they headed off to the café. They were so in love. If only it would be enough to help her through the battles which lay ahead.

Olivia *'tsked tsked'* all morning, with a grin from ear to ear. She was delighted to see her best friend so happy, despite it running alongside the emotional turmoil of losing her mother.

'Pen's farewell was pretty awesome, wasn't it?' Olivia remarked later when they had a quiet lull in the café.

'Yeah, it was. I find it quite incredible what you can learn about a person at their funeral. It's such a shame we don't take the time to really get to know people while they're alive,' she mused, thinking of all the secrets her mother held. 'Clayton and I are heading to Pen's house to do the last of the tidying. Most of his furniture went to charity, but there's personal paperwork to go through now. I'm not looking forward to that. It feels so invasive. It's hard enough going through my mum's stuff, you know.'

'Yeah, but out of everyone Pen knew, he'd have been comfortable with you doing this. You know you were like a daughter to him, Bluey,' Olivia said matter of factly.

Those words caught Bluey right in the throat, and as she tried to tame her rapid breathing, she found Clayton looking at her reassuringly.

They stood on Pen's verandah for some time, looking across the land that had been in his family for generations. Gone. It was all gone now. And to what? Big business? It was all such a terrible waste.

'Clayton, will you come with me on Sunday to meet my grandmother?' she asked out of nowhere. 'It's important to me that she meets you.'

Clayton was deeply moved, just as he had been when Bluey had shared the story of her life, and how her grandmother had held her for a week after her parents' deaths, and at their recent reunion.

'Of course I'll come and meet her,' he promised.

They stepped inside Pen's old house, and surveyed the empty rooms. They were devoid of furniture now, except his bedroom.

Bluey sat on the bed and sighed. 'Do you think they ever made love here?' she said out loud. 'Or do you think it was always at Mum's house?'

'From the way she writes in her diary, Bluey, I'd say it was always at her house. But who knows what happened when you were at school!' he smiled.

'I hate the thought that he slept alone in this bed for all those years. I mean, what happened when I was older? Where did they meet up then? When I was a teenager I was never in bed before midnight,' Bluey stated.

'I'm sure they found their ways. Love always helps you find a way,' Clayton assured her. 'Shall I do this cupboard, and you go through the drawers in the dresser?'

'Yeah,' she sighed, reluctant to go into his personal belongings yet again. 'One day someone's going to be doing this to my things. Making decisions about what to keep, what to throw away,' Bluey said, realising she was on sacred ground.

One by one she took out things from the top drawer. There were bank statements, newspaper clippings of friends who'd made it into the local newspaper for various achievements, unused prescriptions for medication, old books and a small floral-covered box.

She recognised the fabric cover, as it was the same one which lined her mother's wardrobe. 'That's odd,' she said, and proceeded to open it. There were photos of Pen and Bluey playing on the beach, building sandcastles, eating ice cream. In every single photo, Pen Grille was beaming.

She unfolded a piece of paper with a drawing by a

child. It was of a man and a little girl with long blonde pigtails sitting under a gum tree. The word 'daddy' was scribbled on the bottom in a child's scratchy handwriting. On the back was Emily Miller's handwriting: *Bluey drew this in school this morning. Thought you might like it!*

Bluey passed it to Clayton. She didn't need to say anything. He put his arms around her. 'Pen clearly meant a lot more to you when you were a kid than I think your adult self realised,' Clayton whispered, catching her tears on his T-shirt.

'He was always there, you know. I guess something changed as I grew older, and they tried to keep their relationship hidden from me. It's not that he wasn't around then, he was, always...but I just didn't see it for what it was. I guess I was just too caught up in my own dramas: boys, make-up, high heels, food.'

In the bottom drawer were legal documents and assorted paperwork. Bluey stood in stunned silence for a moment, until she fully grasped what she was reading.

'Oh my god!' Bluey blurted out. 'Oh my god!'

'What is it, sweetheart?' Clayton asked, and stopped folding clothes to come and see what had taken her attention.

'I always wondered how my mother afforded to buy the old Cotter house that's now my café. I could never understand how a single mother who sews dresses for a living could buy a house on an acre of land. But she always said she'd been squirreling money away. And I believed her! *Pen gave it to her.* Why didn't he just tell me?' Bluey stood up and walked to the window. 'Why all these secrets? Why couldn't he just say "Bluey, you can have that old house on the bay and convert it into a café"? Why couldn't he tell me?'

'Actions speak louder than words. He lived by that motto, honey. If you focus on the fact they didn't tell you, then you're going to miss out on something so much bigger and better. That man loved you as much as he loved your mother. Can't you see that?' Clayton asked tenderly.

Bluey sobbed into his arms. 'If he loved me so much then why did he sell all his land to Jackson-Briggs? He knew what it would do to me!'

'His dying words were "It's all a mistake. Tell her it's a mistake." I guess he realised a little too late?' Clayton kissed her.

'I had no idea that the café and land deeds were in my name. I just assumed they were all under Mum's name. She always said to leave the rates and water bills and so on to her. So I did! And now I see that this was mine all along and that he was paying for things to make my life easier. I need to go home. I've had enough for one day.'

Clayton drove home slowly. 'Have you given much thought to what you'll do?' he asked as they drove by the beach.

'I don't want to sell, but I don't see I have much choice. Everything that makes the café so wonderful—the location and the isolation from other buildings—well, that will all be gone. It will be stuck in front of a concrete jungle. You know, I get that it's prime real-estate land and perfect for development. What holidaymaker wouldn't want those views of the bay? But does everything natural always have to be destroyed for the benefit of humans?'

'Fancy chips on the beach for dinner,' he asked as they drove passed Henny's Chip Shop.

'Sounds good,' she smiled, grateful for the distraction. 'I'm thinking too much, aren't I?'

Clayton parked the jeep. 'The answers you need aren't going to come from thinking about it, but from following your heart. What does your heart tell you to do?'

They walked across the road to the chip shop.

'My heart says that I'm not going anywhere.' She looked at him thoughtfully. 'It tells me the same thing about you, too,' Bluey smiled, grabbing his hand.

'I could have told your heart that!' he laughed.

'Hey Henny, two bags of chips, and half a dozen pineapple rings, thanks,' Bluey said, grabbing two bottles of apple juice from the fridge.

A few minutes later they were sitting on the sand by the bluff rock, eating chips, laughing, and planning a trip to visit Bluey's grandmother.

The Old Rocking Chair

Clayton and Bluey arrived at Maria Herring's home on Sunday morning, carrying a basket of pineapple and nutmeg muffins. Maria was in her rocking chair on the verandah, reading a book.

'I'm so pleased to meet you, Clayton,' she said warmly, taking his hands in hers, and looking him in the eyes. Bluey hugged her grandmother slowly, and for a long time.

'I brought some muffins for morning tea,' she said proudly.

'Your mother told me you were a wonderful cook,' Maria smiled, taking one from the basket. 'Help yourself to the iced tea.' She pointed to the glass pitcher on the nearby table.

They talked for hours about the café, the changeable weather, Clayton's job, unpacking Pen Grille's home, and about Jackson-Briggs.

'You'll have to be strong and stand your ground,' Maria insisted. 'Just because you're a nice person it doesn't mean you can't be angry or fight for a cause. Even nice people have to say "enough is enough". What have you done to stop these people?' she asked.

'Well, Clayton spent a lot of time negotiating with Pen, but it came to nothing,' Bluey said sadly.

'It wasn't that man you had to negotiate with, it was the big boys. And now it's in their hands, you have to find a way to show them that what they're planning isn't a good idea. Money talks, yes, but even those business men have hearts. You just have to find them,' Maria suggested, as if it were the easiest thing in the world. 'There's something I want to give you, Bluey,' her grandmother confided. 'I probably should have given it to you when you turned eighteen, but you were in a relationship then with someone your mother didn't approve of, and the same at 21, and 23, so I just bided my time. Things are different now, I can see that,' she smiled.

'You knew about Roger?' Bluey asked in disbelief.

'Your mother wrote me weekly letters from the start. I still have a copy of every photo she ever took of you, and of your report cards, and certificates for gymnastics, and piano. Emily was a very good writer, you know. She should have been a novelist instead of a seamstress! Her stories about your adventures were utterly charming. I've kept every single one. Anyway…I'll be back in a minute,' she said, disappearing into the house.

Mrs Herring returned with a folder of papers. 'When your parents died, I inherited their house and savings. I had no need for them, as I already had this place. Emily Miller insisted she didn't need financial help, and that it was wrong for her to take money that wasn't hers. I tried many times over the years to help her out, especially in the tough times, but she wouldn't have a bar of it. I sold the house, and put the money into a high-interest account where it's been growing like a mushroom ever since. It's rightfully yours, Bluey. It won't buy you all of Pen's land back, but you might be able to negotiate with Jackson-Briggs to at least have some buffer land around the café,' she suggested.

Bluey looked from Clayton to her grandmother, and back again. She examined the bank statements, unable to comprehend the wealth in front of her. 'You realise I don't ever have to work again if this money is mine?' Bluey shook her head in disbelief. 'But I love what I do…'

'The money gives you choice, Bluey. It doesn't mean you have to give up your job. It just helps to make life a bit easier,' Clayton said, putting his hand on her lap.

'I can't believe my mother didn't take any of this. If you knew how often she struggled to make ends meet sometimes. Why was she so stubborn?' Bluey growled. She turned to Clayton, 'Do you think Jackson-Briggs would sell a few acres of land to me?'

'We can only try.' He kissed Bluey on her cheek, and then turned to Maria. 'Mrs Herring, Bluey's organised a candlelit supper down at the café next weekend. Would you like me to pick you up? I think you'd really enjoy seeing the life that she's created down in Calico Bay,' he smiled warmly.

'I'd love to!' she said with delight. 'That would be wonderful! I feel like I've been there a thousand times through all the stories Emily wrote me. It would be rather jolly to see it for myself.'

Bluey and Clayton spent the rest of the day with Maria Herring, and then headed home.

Café Blues

Bluey was feeling rather down as another procession of diggers and construction equipment marched its way to Pen Grille's property. Clayton had tried in vain to negotiate with Hugo Briggs and Melvin Jackson. They simply had no interest in ecology, or the conflict their project had with the residents of Calico Bay. Maria Herring was wrong: they didn't have hearts. They only saw dollar signs. Clayton had never come up against such a difficult situation, and out of all the cases he'd ever worked on, this was the one he really didn't want to lose. He owed it to Pen, and he owed it to Bluey.

Jackson-Briggs had sought planning permission several years ago. No one in Calico Bay even objected to it when they saw the plans in the newspaper. They laughed it off. Pen Grille would never sell up to big business. Everyone knew that! The local council might have been fooled into believing it would be good for the economy and local area, but the residents knew it would never happen.

Clayton broke the news as gently to Bluey as possible, but it didn't stop her feeling sad. 'I'm sorry honey, I tried everything I could,' he said, holding her close, and kissing her brow.

She'd closed the café early so she could prep for tonight's candlelit supper. They had full numbers booked, and Clayton had promised to bring his guitar and sing. He sat in the corner practising a few pieces, looking up from time to time just to keep an eye on Bluey. He knew how vulnerable she was feeling. A while later, when Olivia came in to help, Clayton drove to Maria Herring's house to pick her up.

As evening settled, the townsfolk gathered on the verandah and indoors at Bluey's Café. Bluey had lit dozens of beeswax candles, their gentle honey scent wafting through the café. Twelve lanterns were lit on the verandah. Tonight's food was a simple help-yourself set menu:

Moroccan chickpea and apricot soup
Red capsicum stuffed with basmati rice,
black olives and cherry tomatoes
Mushroom terrine
Cashew and red wine moussaka
Emily Miller's chocolate pudding

Clayton licked his fingers after wiping the remains of his pudding bowl.

'Did your mum teach you to cook?' he asked, as she sat on his lap after dinner.

'No, she taught me to sew! When I was 18, I went overseas for a few weeks to India to volunteer in an orphanage. Afterwards, I stayed with a family, and learnt to cook Indian food from them. The next year, I went to South Africa, and did the same thing: a few weeks in an orphanage, and then a week with a local family learning to cook. And East Africa, Jamaica, Thailand… Every year, I went to another country and volunteered time with the orphans, and then I'd come back with new recipe ideas.'

'Bluey, that's amazing. Why haven't you ever told me that before?' Clayton asked, flabbergasted that she'd not shared such an important part of her life.

'I've had a lot on my mind lately!' she reminded him. 'I'm thinking of going to Sri Lanka in five months. You could join me...' she said, putting the thought out there; daring to tempt fate and their future by thinking so far ahead.

He didn't answer, but asked 'Why the orphanages? Do you feel you owe something because of your start in life?'

'Well, I don't feel obligated. I feel blessed. Out of all the women in the world, I got Emily for my mum. Most of those kids will never have a mother. I just want to spend time with them. Give them some love. I know what good mother-love feels like. I've had a lifetime of it. I just want to share it around. Everyone in this bay jokes that I'll never have babies because I've been so crap in relationships...' she laughed. 'I shouldn't tell you that, should I? But there's no reason I can't spend time with these kids; and you know, it benefits me as much as them.'

'Let's prove them wrong,' Clayton said seriously, holding her close. He nuzzled into her neck, and said 'I want to have babies with you.'

She looked up at him, and realised he was serious.

'Hey Clayton, aren't you supposed to be singing tonight,' Olivia joshed, breaking up the intimate moment.

'Yes I am,' he laughed, reluctantly letting go of Bluey and getting his guitar from the kitchen. But his eyes never left her as he watched her take in the last words of their conversation. He started to sing:

> *You're just too good to be true*
> *Can't take my eyes off of you*
> *You'd be like heaven to touch*
> *I wanna hold you so much*
> *At long last love has arrived*
> *And I thank God I'm alive*
> *You're just too good to be true*
> *Can't take my eyes off of you...*

Bluey felt the colour rush to her cheeks. Her emotional life was like a roller coaster right now. Up one minute, down the next, changing direction here, there and everywhere: giddy, laughing, scared. But through it all, Clayton was there, holding her hand on the roller coaster, promising that she was safe.

Maria Herring had a wonderful evening at the café, getting to know more about Bluey's life, and meeting her friends; but for the past half hour she'd been in deep conversation with Matt Stonebrook, a man two years her junior. Her eyes were sparkling, and she was laughing freely.

'I can't believe how much you look like your grandmother,' Olivia whispered to Bluey.

'What, the grey hair, wrinkles, dodgy knees?'

'Well, it's like you've come from the same cookie cutter. At least I know what you'll look like in fifty years!' Olivia laughed. 'How does it feel having her in your life again? She must be like a complete stranger?' she probed.

'Actually, oddly enough, it's like I've always known her,' she said, and then shared her faded memory of being held in a rocking chair and cuddled for days on end.

'Wow, that's not something you'd forget in a hurry. It's a shame she lives over an hour away. I'd bet she'd really love living that bit closer,' Olivia said, wondering what it might be like for Bluey to have some blood family nearby.

'That has crossed my mind. I haven't said anything to her because everything's so up in the air about the café. I'm determined to stand my ground here, but I may not be so sure once the trees come down and I'm staring at acre upon acre of concrete jungle,' Bluey lamented. 'Look at her! Is she? No… she can't be! Is she actually *flirting*?' she asked in disbelief.

'Well, let's hope she has better luck in the men department than you Bluey Miller! Though I have to say, things have looked rather different for you these past few weeks. Clayton is completely different to any guy you've ever gone out with before!'

'And that has made all the difference,' she smiled, wondering what she could do to ensure he never left her side. Bluey watched him entertain folks with his warm baritone voice, and gentle smile. His banter between songs always led to a hushed silence amongst the crowd. She watched his suntanned hands strum the guitar strings, and she fell in love all over again. Dizzy with joy, she sighed. *Is this real? Is he real?*

Clayton continued to play familiar ballads, and everyone sang along. There was much dancing and laughter, and despite all the recent pain in her life, Bluey found herself feeling happy.

At just after midnight, Bluey brought Clayton another glass of wine and asked 'Shall we do a duet?'

She settled into the chair beside him, and to the melody of Red Dirt, they sang:

The scent of sweet Sun on your skin,
Leaves me weak, draws me in
And I am falling, I am falling, and I am falling fast.

I feel the beating of your heart,
Every breath lights up the dark
And I am longing, I am longing
Longing for your touch.

Red dirt, blue skies
You leave me nowhere else to hide.
Red dirt, blue skies, hello to you my sweet surprise.

Trembling I stand in awe
Feel the healing, feel the force
And we are flying, we are flying
And we are flying free.

I give to you my heart, my soul
I give our story not yet told
We are soaring, we are soaring,
We're soaring heaven high.

Red dirt, blue skies
You leave me nowhere else to hide
Red dirt, blue skies, hello to you my sweet surprise.

An Empty House

Bluey stood on the verandah of Pen's old Queenslander, surveying the land around her.

'This is just so wrong,' she said out loud. She walked down the wooden steps into the garden, and out the back of the bungalow. The vegetable beds were past their sell-by date, and most of the produce had gone to seed from too much heat and no watering. Bluey wiped her tears. He'd looked after this family home for all of his adult life. It was designed to raise a family in, and had done so for generations. And now it was to be bulldozed to the ground. It was just so wrong!

She had come to say one last goodbye to the place, and found herself wandering into the bush, breathing in the early morning scent of the earth, and taking in the sound of the dawn chorus. *More like an out-of-tune orchestra*, with each bird competing to be the loudest, she thought to herself.

The sunshine-yellow wattle and crimson-coloured bottlebrush were in full bloom, and there was life all around her.

Pen Grille had deliberately kept this native bush intact, ensuring the sanctity of the ecology of Calico Bay was honoured. Bluey once heard her mother mention that Pen wanted to put it into trust to ensure it could never be destroyed.

'What happened, old fella?' she asked softly into the morning air. 'Did your heart break so much that you just gave up?'

Bluey sat on the ground and wept. Had she been responsible in some way for the upcoming demise of this land? Was it her fault that Pen Grille and Emily Miller didn't get married? Was it because of her that Pen Grille was now lying in the ground having died from a broken heart?

It was all too much to bear. Bluey felt safe out here in the bush, and she let the native flora and fauna hold her for the longest time. Grief poured out of her body, washing itself into the soil. Kookaburras mocked her, and laughed their message: *if you're going to cry, then just get on with it.*

Later, she heard a car pull up in Pen's driveway, and looked over to see Clayton in his jeep. Bluey dusted herself off, then ran over, and fell into his arms.

'Honey, I'm here now. Just let it all out.'

And she did. Her wailing continued unabated and uncensored.

When she finally composed herself, Bluey said 'This is such a beautiful house. It deserves to be lived in and enjoyed, not flattened to the ground!'

'I know,' he said, comforting her physically, and knowing there was absolutely nothing he could do to soften the emotional pain.

'Pen was at every important event of my life. How have I not seen the significance of that? How did my mother not see it? Or maybe she did. Maybe she was always wanting the adult me to say something.'

'You can't keep doing these "what ifs?" and beating yourself up. Neither of them would want that for you. They really wouldn't. Bluey, they truly loved each other, and they made sure they spent time together. Their relationship might not have been conventional in that it wasn't out in the open, but that doesn't make it any less real. From what we've read in your mum's diary, their love was more real than just about any married couple I know. That is what you've got to hold in your memory.'

His sage words wrapped themselves around her, as if she were the finest gift in the land: pretty paper, silky ribbon, and a beautiful bow to both celebrate and protect the precious contents.

She kissed him softly, and then said 'I have no idea how I'd have survived these past few weeks without you. You've changed my life.' She smiled, shocked at the reality of the situation.

'I need to head back home tomorrow and sort through some things. I probably won't be back up here for another week,' he said, breaking the news softly.

'Okay,' Bluey replied, trying to be brave, but feeling like she'd topple over at any minute. 'Okay.'

'But for today, I'm all yours. Later, I need to go through and sort Pen's old shed. There's some really valuable woodturning equipment in there. Let's go and take a walk through this land one last time.'

Sniffing away her tears, Bluey took Clayton's hand in hers, and they walked on through the bush for several minutes. It was going to be another scorcher, and already the trees offered a semblance of cool shade.

Pen had almost two hundred acres of native scrubland, and in parts it was quite thick and impenetrable. In other places, the trees were sparse. From time to time, they came across well-worn paths firmly etched into the red soil by rabbits and kangaroos, and probably by Pen himself.

'He's managed this quite well you know, considering his age,' Clayton said, 'Not bad at all.'

'How could he have had such an about-turn and want to sell this?' Bluey asked, still utterly bewildered by his change of heart.

'Honey, he was a broken man. Broken men don't think straight. He went to his grave regretting signing the property over to Jackson-Briggs. You have to know that,' Clayton said firmly.

'I do....I just wish I could change things. I want to make things better. To go back in time,' she insisted, kicking the soil.

'Sometimes you've got to let go of the idea of good and bad, and accept that things just happen, and that we have to make choices,' he said, trying to comfort her torment caused from over-thinking.

They came to a small pond, fed from a nearby secret

spring, which trickled over mossy granite rocks, and was shrouded by delicate maidenhair ferns.

'I've walked this land for my entire childhood, and I've never seen this before,' Bluey said, and was utterly speechless for the next few minutes. 'It's beautiful. How have I not seen this before? I thought I'd walked every square inch of this land.'

'Hey, look at this!' Clayton called over to her. He had discovered a hand-carved sculpted figure, made of wood, and hidden near the mouth of the spring. Clayton ran his hands over the worn wood, admiring Pen's perfectionist woodwork.

'Oh my god, that's my *mother*!'

They both stood in awe at the accuracy to detail.

'What's that?' Clayton wondered, spying a small box, about a metre high, made from corrugated iron and wood. Bluey followed him over, and they opened it.

Inside were pillows and blankets, and bottles of red wine, and glasses.

Bluey and Clayton looked at each other in amazement.

'They were lovers right to the end, Bluey. Well, at least until your mother got too ill to come here,' Clayton suggested. 'This is where they came to be lovers.'

'By why didn't they just do it in the house?' Bluey asked, confused by the elaborate hiding of this lovers' nest.

'Did you ever go to Pen's house?' Clayton asked.

'Of course I did. All the time. I had a key. He used to always be fixing things for me, or I'd pop by with clothes Mum had repaired, or muffins I'd baked,' she said, not realising exactly what she was saying.

'That's why they made love out here!' Clayton laughed out loud. 'They didn't want Miss Bluey Know-it-All Miller walking in on them!'

'Oh…' she said, slowing taking in the fact her mother had a secret love-making place out amongst the trees. 'Oh…' and then she burst out laughing. 'I really didn't know my mother at all, did I?' she smiled, enjoying the thought of Emily and Pen's secret trysts! 'But this place would have meant the world to him. Why would he then give it away?'

'Because his world was gone, Bluey,' Clayton said kindly. 'She was gone.'

Bluey pulled the sheets, blankets and pillows out of the tin box, and opened the wine. 'Not too early for a glass of red, is it?' she teased, but before she could pour any, Clayton had taken her in his arms. Caressing her affectionately, his body invited her to come closer. His shirt was discarded, and so were his jeans. Her dress followed them, dropped with a wild abandon on the woodland floor of dirt and eucalyptus leaves and gumnuts.

But what began urgently, like a highly spiced hot rumba, soon settled into the pleasure of listening to Debussy's *Au Claire De Lune* on a rainy Sunday afternoon. It was something to be enjoyed slowly, mindfully: every second becoming a lifetime. The best music was always enjoyed without distraction. Unforbidden pleasure beckoned them to each other, once again. Their bodies were right: there was no hurry. There was nowhere they had to be. Just here, just now; beneath the trees.

A dog barking in the distance, a rosella in a nearby tree, and the stream trickling over ancient granite, were the only sounds around, apart from their moans of pleasure. They were at home in each other's arms, and each time they loved in this way, Clayton felt Bluey unfold more into her body, unashamedly offering herself up for more. Softening, yielding, wanting.

Clayton's body was warm, and his natural body odour reminded her of the earthy spice, cumin. It made her want more. And, just as in the kitchen, she breathed in deeply, her body enchanted by the age-old joy of being human: food and lovemaking, the staples of life.

They made love until mid-afternoon, and fell asleep under the trees. When they awoke, some time later, Bluey said, 'That could become addictive.'

She smiled, as they lay in each other's arms, content with the world.

Discovery

The morning air tangoed with the aroma of freshly ground Arabic coffee beans. Clayton lounged in one of the armchairs in the café's bookshop area, drinking an Americano, and reading through Bluey's collection of recipes. With his mouth watering, he immersed himself in her rich culinary vocabulary: page after page of delicious and stylish recipes, drawings, anecdotes and photos from her various foreign travels. The abundant collection of recipes was a testament to the pleasure of food: growing, preparing, sharing and eating it. Clayton was glued to the pages; it read like a novel: fast and pacey, in parts; then slow and seductive. Thoughtful, honest, revealing, insightful.

The wooden sign, *Artisan Boulanger*, hung from a black wrought-iron hanger, and swung gently in the breeze. Clayton found himself standing outside the small family bakery in a tiny French village, seeing life through the eyes of twenty-three-year old Bluey. She'd volunteered for two weeks with the Dubois family, and her writings spoke of discovering good hand-crafted bread: texture, feel, fragrance, flavour and colour. *Bread is art*, Old Man Dubois had told Bluey, as he mentored her through the ancient skills of kneading and fermenting, instilling patience in her restless body.

Each morning, she would dress the bakery window: hessian bags of flour, ears of wheat, cob loaves and plaits, or wildflowers she'd gathered while on her walks in the morning. Within the wooden, curtained alcove, she'd carefully arrange loaves and wreaths on wooden racks, and marvelled at the social rituals observed around bread. Bluey's baking repertoire expanded. She soon learnt that many of the old baker's customers came by twice a day to ensure they always had the freshest of bread.

An in-depth description of making almond croissants

from scratch—the smell of marzipan and the feel of flaked almonds in her palms—had Clayton getting up from his comfy armchair and heading into the kitchen. 'I'm hungry!'

Bluey laughed, and said 'That'll teach you for reading my recipes!'

He snatched a piece of pear and ginger cake from the cooling rack when her back was turned, and returned to the comfort of his velvet-covered chair to continue reading: it was a lazy Sunday afternoon in an outdoor café in Greece. On the table before her, a feast: hommous, stuffed vine leaves, grilled vegetables, followed by bruschetta with tomatoes and mushrooms. And then, ragout with green beans, potatoes and tomatoes. The man on the balalaika, plucking the strings softly at the door to the café, asked Bluey if she had a favourite tune.

Clayton called out to the kitchen: 'How much food did you eat in Greece?'

She laughed in response. 'Not nearly enough! It was all just research, you know.'

Clayton thought about the expansive walk-in pantry in Bluey's Café, and how the wooden shelves were stocked high with imported olive oils, squat glass jars brimming with char-grilled marinated artichokes, olives and sun-dried tomatoes in oil. He thought about the focaccia bread she'd made last week, and the fresh rosemary, olives, sun-dried tomatoes and sea salt on top. Clayton discovered so much about his beloved Bluey by seeing the world through her eyes: eyes that loved food, eyes that loved life.

As he read about the citrus trees in Spain, and how enchanted Bluey was by the lavender fields of Provence, the terracotta rooftops of Italy, and the olive groves, Clayton became aware that this was one of her few travels which didn't mention a man. *Hmmm*, he thought to himself. *All alone beneath those blue skies?*

'So, no love interest on your holiday in the

Mediterranean then?' Clayton asked curiously, taking a mouthful of *kulfi*, Indian mango icecream, when he returned to the kitchen.

'You'll just never know,' she teased, and he tickled her for a confession, but there wasn't one.

A Long Week

Clayton had been gone for four days, and to Bluey it felt like the longest four days of her life. She just didn't feel the same without him nearby, even though he phoned three times a day!

Bluey woke up early, and instead of getting dressed, she opened her mother's diary.

Dear diary...
I'm concerned about Bluey. I really don't like this guy she's dating. Roger is everything I don't want her to have in a boyfriend. At one level, I know it's none of my business, but at another I feel so utterly protective of her. Pen even said today, "I don't like that boy. I don't trust him". Well, I nearly fell over backwards to hear Pen say so much in one go!

I can't put my finger on it. It's not that he's done or said anything, it's just a mother's gut instinct. I don't like him! But, she's eighteen in two months. An adult! Or so she keeps reminding me every time she says she's old enough to do what she wants. I have to admit to finding this age to be the toughest of all in which to parent. Bluey will be a woman in her own right, and it's up to her who she dates. I still feel like putting poison in his coffee though! I hate the way he saunters around this house like a tomcat, sniffing out the territory. I do everything I can to make sure they're not left alone together.

Two months later...
I knew he couldn't be trusted! This morning she cried solidly in my arms for three hours.

I've never seen her howl like that. She was so distressed I wanted to call the doctor and get her sedated.

Roger had wanted sex last night, and said he couldn't wait any longer. He threatened to dump her if she didn't "go all the way". She replied, "Dump me then", and laughed. His reply was to slap her across the face, and he kicked her to the ground.

He got on his motorbike and just left her at the North Hebiji beach line; two hours walk away! But then he came back, and tried to force himself on her. She screamed and kicked, and finally she bit him so hard on the shoulder that he yelped with pain and left her alone. The damage had been done though. Bluey might not have had sex, but he interfered with her severely.

I can't imagine that she'll ever trust a man again. I promise her that we're going to go straight to the police and have him charged. She begged me not to...she doesn't want the town to think she's "loose". She said that they won't understand...that they wouldn't believe her. Bluey said that every girl her age has had sex, and no one will believe that she didn't want to. They'll say she consented. I tried to tend to her bruises with arnica cream, and soothe the blisters on her feet from the long walk home. If I ever see Roger Willets again, I swear I'll kill him with my bare hands. For now, though, the only thing I can do is to just keep on loving her.

Bluey shuddered as she relived the trauma of that night. Roger had told everyone in town that he'd had it off with

Bluey, and what a little tart she was. *An easy lay*, he said. Bluey had known she should have told everyone the truth; that she should have reported him to the police, but all she wanted to do was hide away. And so she did. She got together her savings from working at Henny's Chip Shop, and booked an overseas holiday with Volunteers Abroad.

Now her heart was pounding in her chest, like a police officer banging on the front door before a raid. She thought about Roger's rough handling, and how he'd brutally beat her with a stick. Instinctively, Bluey placed her hands between her legs as she relived the trauma of one of the worst nights of her life.

Wincing at the powerful memories now tormenting her, she recalled her mother sensitively and gently tending to her private areas, and mending them with the most delicate of stitching. Her mother had cursed, and said "I'm a seamstress, not a surgeon!" Over and over she pleaded, "Let me drive you to a doctor".

But Bluey had begged her not to take her to the hospital. And so, morning and night, her mother bathed her grazes with calendula tincture, and rubbed arnica cream into the dozens of bruises. Every day, her mother nurtured her back to health.

At that moment, Clayton crossed her mind. The way he had touched her was so soft, kind, gentle and respectful, that she never even thought of Roger during the past few weeks. The experiences were incomparable, until now. Until now, as she reread the horror of her 18th birthday.

One month later...
I swore to Bluey that I'd never tell anyone what happened, but Pen knew something was irrevocably wrong in our home. He could feel it. That man knew me inside out, and there was no way I was going to be able to keep fobbing him off every night.

I swore him to secrecy. When I told him exactly what Roger had done to Bluey, he sat and cried in my arms. "Our girl" was all he said, but he cried like a baby into the early hours of the morning.

Another month later...
Roger hasn't been seen by anyone for a few weeks. Someone said he'd moved to Western Australia, but there hasn't been a trace of him. I'm glad. Not that Bluey would be tempted back, not after her experience. She doesn't even go out with her friends to the beach at night anymore. I fear she has emotional scars for life. I only wish I could describe to her how beautiful a loving relationship can be: that not all men are bastards!

I asked Pen about Roger, but he just raised his eyebrows and shrugged his shoulders. "Good riddance" was all he said. I'm not going to ask any more questions. Some things are best left unsaid.

Bluey leaves for India tomorrow. This will be our first time apart, and I'm so nervous. She might be an adult, but she'll always be my little girl. Always! Her bags are packed. The orphanage is on the outskirts of Chennai. My tears won't stop. Pen said he'd drive us to the airport. He knows I'll be in no state to do it myself.

The next few pages of the diary were filled with postcards from Chennai. Bluey relived her first overseas experience, and was back on the beach with the orphans, eating tropical fruits, and dancing on the sand. She laughed to see her handwriting, and the passionate words on each postcard. *They were the best days,* she said to herself. *The best!*

Pen has moved in while Bluey is overseas. It feels so right, so natural having him here, but I know it would be different if Bluey was here too. I don't want her to feel she has to move out. This is her home, it always has been. But oh how I'm loving these days. I miss Bluey terribly, and can't wait for her to come home...to be back safe here with me.

Pen and I usually make love about three times a day. I have to remind him that I have jobs to do. And so does he. I often wonder if we'd been together before I met Bluey, how different things might have been: had we all started life together as a family, instead of this silly secretive life I live.

Bluey closed her eyes. *What a love affair Pen and Emily had!,* she thought to herself. Her mind went to Clayton. She was missing him terribly.

Bluey's been back a week. The change in her is incredible. I don't know if she's deliberately blocked out what happened with Roger, or if she's just making a concerted effort to get on with her life, but she is glowing. I can't get her out of my kitchen, though, and it smells of curry at all hours of the day: korma, balti, tandoori, Madras. There are handmade naan breads and poppadoms, mango chutney and pineapple relishes, too. The house is like an Indian restaurant, but without all the diners to consume the vast quantities she's cooking up.

Bluey wants to open a café. My heart sinks. These things cost money, and my savings are limited. I think of asking Maria Herring for the money that she's got in trust for Bluey, but change my mind. Bluey's in such a great place right now that I dare not open the wound of her adoption. My hands are tied. I complain to Pen about my desperation to help Bluey achieve her dream. He finishes the last bowl of tandoori that Bluey had made earlier, wipes his mouth, and says "I'm off", and heads out the door. For the first time in our relationship I actually find myself thinking "You rude man!"

Three weeks later...
Pen phoned and said, "Come over, as soon as you can", and then hung up. I tried not to fume at his lack of social skills, and drove on over. He was sitting on the verandah, with a cup of tea, and a huge smile on his face. Pen handed me a piece of paper: deeds to an acre of land and the old abandoned Cotter House down on the shoreline that belonged to his grandmother.

"This is for Bluey. Don't tell her it came from me. I'll get some blokes in to knock a few walls down so she can make it into a café, and we'll fix up the verandah. No point that building going to waste. She'll pick up the passing tourists, there, too. Calico Bay could do with some of her good cooking. Already spoke to the chaps at the council. There's no problem getting permission to change its use from a house to a business. Cup of tea?" I stood there, speechless. Talk about a change of roles. He said more in the past thirty seconds than he had in the past thirty years! Why was he doing this?

Bluey sat on the bed crying. *He loved me like I was his own child*, she sobbed into the pillow. *He loved me!*

Two months later...
Bluey opened Bluey's Café today! There can't
have been a single person who didn't come
by and either have a bowl of Madras curry or
chickpea and capsicum korma. She's figured out
that she can't run the café on her own, not if
it was ever going to get as busy as it did today.
Olivia was at her side all day, making coffees,
serving tea, bringing out home-made lemonade.
Bluey's hired her to work full-time. It's a huge
venture for both of them, but today they looked
so happy. Pen came by late in the day, had a
cup of tea, and said "Well done, girl", and then
left. I know he's so proud of her.

Three months later...
Bluey said that Pen comes by the café every day
at 2.30pm, and has a pot of tea and a pumpkin
scone. He prefers to visit at the back-end of the
day when the lunch crowd has gone, and it's
a bit quieter. He always asks what sort of day
she's had, and the last thing he says every time
he walks out the front door to leave is "Are you
happy?" Bluey said that she's glad he asks this,
even though it seems a bit odd to ask the same
question five days a week. It reminds her that
this is such a fabulous time in her life. She feels
creative, expansive, and is having lots of fun.
"Mum, I'm very happy" she said, hugging me
tight today.

Dot the 'I's and Cross the 'T's

Hart turned up at the café at 6.15am.

'I'm sorry for coming by so early when you're trying to get ready, but I couldn't wait any longer,' he said excitedly.

'I've been going through the copies of the paperwork for the Jackson-Briggs deal. Pen didn't sign them! He didn't write his name on there. He signed *Emily Miller*!' Hart said, jumping up and down with excitement, rather uncharacteristically.

'What do you mean he signed *Emily Miller*?' Bluey begged to know.

'I think his mind was elsewhere, and he just wasn't thinking. Look, I don't know if this was accidental or deliberate. Those hounds were on his back night and day for years trying to get a signature. Maybe he just scribbled something to shut them up, but they didn't look very closely. Bluey, these documents are invalid without his signature. I have to declare them null and void. I just wanted to come and tell you before I phone Jackson-Briggs and put a stop to the development.'

She stood in stunned silence for several minutes.

'What happens to the land now?' Bluey asked, still not comprehending this latest news.

'Can you come to my office?' he asked, dodging her question.

'Now? Um, okay. Let me phone Olivia and get her to come in early.'

Ten minutes later Bluey was sitting across from Hart at his desk.

'Take a look at this,' he said, passing over the last will and testament of his friend, Pen Grille. It was dated six months ago. 'He came in and made this after he found out about your mother's illness.'

*I hereby bequeath my entire estate to Bluey (Maria)
Anastasia Miller, including two hundred acres of
native scrubland, my house, and my woodturning
business. All funds in my bank account at the time of
my death are also bequeathed to her.*

'Hart, what does this mean?' she asked, not taking in the magnitude of the morning's news.

'It means, firstly, there's no development; and secondly, it means that his house and the entire spread of land of Calico Bay behind Bluey's Café, is now yours. There'll be some paper work to do which could take me a couple of weeks, but from this moment, legally, it's all yours,' he smiled, knowing it couldn't have gone to a nicer person.

Her life flashed before her. There were so many decisions to make. What would she do with so much land? And what about the old farmhouse? The one she'd just emptied out! All that furniture she'd given to charity! She sighed, and said, 'I just can't take all this in.'

'It's a lot to digest. I suggest you just carry on as normal for now. There's no need for big decisions just yet. You've already got the keys to Pen's house. Why don't you head back there and see it through new eyes,' he encouraged. 'See it through *your* eyes.'

'He really loved my mum, Hart. Really loved her,' she said, tears slipping fast down her cheeks.

'I know dear. I know. He was in love with her since primary school. He told me very early on that he'd never love another woman. It was only ever her. But you know, it's not true. There *was* another woman,' he smiled.

'There was?' she asked incredulously, fearing their great love affair was about to be tarnished.

'He loved *you*. He told me once that you were the daughter he never had.'

She left his office in tears, and walked back to the café.

Driving Lessons

Bluey needed to pick up some extra vegetables for the café, and for the first time since her mother's death, got into her mum's car. She sat there for a while, breathing in the smell of her mother's perfume. Her thoughts turned to the time her mother tried to give her a driving lesson. It was disastrous. They both came home with a headache, and Emily Miller vowed never to get in the car again if Bluey was at the wheel. Pen's response was: 'I'll teach her.'

Bluey had loved her lessons with Pen. Every afternoon he took her onto the rough dirt tracks on his land, and gave Bluey a hands-off approach to learning. He let her put her foot down, and taught her how an engine worked, and how to change the oil and tyres.

'Oh Pen,' she whispered, sniffing back her tears. 'You were so very good to me. Why didn't I ever take the time to tell you that?'

She started the engine, and let it warm up. Flicking on the radio, she hummed to the old Carly Simon song, *Nothing Stays the Same*. 'That's for sure. Who's going to teach me to drive now, Pen?' she said out loud. 'There are all these roads which lie before me, and I don't know how to drive them or which one to follow!' Bluey hung her head low and wept.

Later, Bluey stopped by Reg Varney's Veg Shop, and picked up root and salad vegetables. In her basket, she gathered together some fresh herbs: coriander, parsley, mint, borage and basil.

'What's on the menu this week?' Reg asked as he wrote out the invoice.

He was a regular diner at the café, and always marvelled at how she transformed his produce.

'Good question! To be honest, I have no idea. Guess

I'll have to surprise you,' she winked, and headed back to the other end of the bay.

Bluey's Café sat alone against the backdrop of two-hundred acres of native bushland. She stayed in the car for the longest time looking at the view to either side of her. Her life, which had felt like it was closing down before her, was suddenly opening up in ways she could never have imagined. Contraction. Expansion. Like labour and birth.

She thought of Clayton, and wondered where and how he would fit into the picture. One thing was for sure, she couldn't imagine him not being here.

Carrying boxes of produce into the café kitchen, Bluey told Olivia of the news. They hugged and laughed and cried.

'Good old Penrith Ebeneezer Grille! Who'd have thought that old codger would have the last laugh? You're not going to take the money and run, are you?' Olivia asked suspiciously.

'No, Liv, I'm not,' Bluey promised.

It was a little after 3pm, when a familiar jeep pulled up outside the café. Bluey ran outside, and straight into Clayton's embrace. 'I thought you were never coming back,' she whispered.

'Are you kidding? Nothing could keep me away.' He lifted her off the ground, and kissed her cheek. 'I hoped I'd get here before you shut...Too late for coffee?'

'You could never be too late,' she smiled, leading him up the stairs.

As they sat down and sipped coffee, and shared a slice of Black Forest cake, Bluey told him all of her news.

'That sly old fox!' Clayton laughed out loud, slapping his hands on the table with joy. 'You know, the number of times he said to me that it was your land, and I wondered if he was going senile...'

'He said that to you?' she asked, in shock.

'Yeah, I didn't say anything because it just felt so far removed from what was happening with Jackson-Briggs and Sandler's trying to negotiate. I didn't know where his comments fitted in to all that. Now I do!'

'You think he put my mum's signature there on purpose?'

'Bloody oath! Of course he did.'

They sat in silence for some time, just enjoying seeing each other's face again.

'I've had an idea,' she confided. 'Actually, I've had so many ideas today that I've nearly given myself a headache.'

'Tell me,' he encouraged.

'Pen's house...' she started to say.

'You need to stop calling it Pen's house, Bluey. It's yours now.' Clayton smiled, reaching over for her hand.

'My house,' she corrected herself with a giggle, 'is in need of a good coat of paint, and that vegetable garden needs some serious work... but I think it would be perfect for my grandmother. She'd be close by, and wouldn't be so alone. I also think that top field by the Briar Ridge would make an excellent little market garden...' She was talking so fast that Clayton could hardly keep up. 'When I was a teenager, I worked at Henny's Chip Shop, part time. It wasn't the greatest job in the world, what with smelly, pimply teenage boys leering at me, but it was so wonderful to be able to earn my own money. Well, if I set up that field for vegetable growing, I could hire a few teenagers to maintain it... It could be a little market garden, run as a cooperative. They wouldn't just learn how to grow vegetables, but about marketing and money management.'

'That sounds like a brilliant idea,' Clayton smiled, warming to her enthusiasm. 'Have you given any thought to the woodturning tools in his shed?'

'What? You mean *my* shed?' she laughed. 'No, I'd

forgotten about them.'

'Well, in that rusty old tin shed are a hell of a lot of expensive tools. I did a fair bit of woodturning when I was younger. It wouldn't take long to brush up my skills. We could sell some pieces here, and even teach some of those teenagers how to turn wood,' Clayton said enthusiastically. But he couldn't say another word because Bluey was straight on his lap and kissing him.

'Perfect. It's perfect!' she laughed, and then sadness sank across her face like the fading light of day. 'But how will you have time to do that, do your job and come and visit me on weekends?' she asked.

'Visit you on weekends? I hadn't planned on doing that.'

Confusion washed over Bluey's face.

'Honey, I work freelance. I'm free to visit you every day of the week.'

'You are! But what are you going to do for a job?' She was desperate for answers.

'It sounds like you're going to have enough work around here to keep me busy. That is, if you want me to do it?' he hesitated.

'Want you? Are you kidding? I'd love you to be here. Would you be able to look after all of Pen's land—*my* land—and do woodturning?'

'Yep, and I could probably supervise a few randy teenagers while they're digging up potatoes, too.'

'Clayton, this all feels like a dream. A dream I don't ever want to wake up from.'

'Who says you have to?' He kissed her lovingly. 'I've rented out my house in Toowoomba, but I haven't got anywhere else lined up yet. Perhaps I could stay at Pen's while we fix it up?' he suggested.

'No, that won't work at all!' she insisted. 'You can move in with me and commute to Pen's...to *my* house! We really need to give that place a name!' she laughed. 'I want to show it to grandmother. Shall we go and get her?'

'Why don't you let me paint it first, and tidy up the garden. Just in case she doesn't have a good imagination,' he warned, good-humouredly. 'It is pretty run-down!'

Bluey quickly agreed, and then dragged him out the front of the café, locking the doors behind her.

'Where are we going?' he quizzed her, watching the determined expression on her face.

'To the hardware store. We've got paint to buy! Can I drive?' she asked. 'I've never driven a jeep before,' she said, and he chucked her his keys.

Two kilometres later, and Clayton couldn't help asking, 'Who the hell taught you to drive?'

'Penrith Ebeneezer Grille,' she said proudly. 'Did a great job, didn't he? This is so much fun!' she laughed, as the sea breeze blew her long blonde hair in all directions.

'This is the reason you ride a scooter, isn't it?' he laughed, holding tight to the dashboard. 'So that there's a limit to how fast you can go?'

'Yeah, it was Pen's idea. He gave it to me for my twenty-first birthday.

A Fresh Start

For five solid days, from dawn to dusk, Clayton Lansen worked at Pen's old place. He painted the walls of the old farmhouse, and at sundown he took a break, and played around in the shed with the wood-turning equipment. When Bluey turned up later that week and found him in the shed, he said 'Have a look at this!' and showed her a beautiful hand-crafted coffee table.

'Do you think your grandmother will like it?' he asked.

Bluey cried. 'Clayton, it's beautiful. Simply beautiful. Wow. You really do need to make furniture like this to sell at the café. The tourists will snap them up.'

Clayton smiled and said, 'Come inside. It's looking much better.'

She followed him indoors, and marvelled at the transformation. 'I picked up some more paints. I hope you don't mind. It's so boring painting in white for hours at a time,' he said. But Bluey was too busy admiring the colourful palette as she wandered from room to room. The kitchen, which overlooked a dam, was now Russian-velvet pink.

'I'll make some curtains to match,' Bluey smiled, knowing just the fabric to use. The dining room was sunflower yellow, and the bathroom was lilac. Clayton had brought some peace lilies for the window ledge. It was looking like a home already.

Granny's bedroom was soft magnolia, and the other bedrooms were baby blue and lavender.

'This is so amazing. I could move right in myself. It's wonderful! When can we bring her down?' Bluey asked impatiently.

'Now, if you want; but I'd really like to spend a couple of days doing the garden. Can you wait that long? I know you're so keen to bring her here, but it'd be great if everything was ready.'

'You're right. I'll be patient!' she said, holding his hand. 'What if she says no? What if she doesn't want to move? I mean, she's lived in that house for most of her life. And, to be honest, she doesn't really know me yet. It's a big ask.'

'If she says no, then you can rent it out. Or, we could move in ourselves. One bridge at a time, hey?' He held her close. 'Fancy a little walk?' he asked.

'Sure, where to?'

He started singing the old country-music song, *Blanket on the Ground*.

'Clayton Lansen, what have you got in mind?' she teased.

'I think you know,' he laughed, and they raced each other to the old spring, and pulled out the blankets. Making themselves a comfortable bed under the trees, they held each other as the Sun went down, and beneath the stars they made love. It was as if it was the first time: full of excitement, nervousness and pleasurable intensity; but it was also as if they'd made love to each other a thousand times before: familiar, comfortable, safe and deeply loving.

Sated, she asked: 'Are you really here to stay? You're not going away anymore?'

'I'm here to stay. Where else could I be? What we have, Bluey, it comes along once in a lifetime, and then, only if you're lucky. Only if you're in the right place at the right time.'

'I've got so much to thank Pen for: the way he loved my mother, the way he loved me,' she reflected. 'This land, my café; but out of all of it, he brought you into my life. He gave me you.' She smiled, tracing her fingers down the side of Clayton's muscular, tanned back.

'Well, there's only one thing for it Miss Miller. Let me make love to you again, and dedicate this one to Pen Grille,' he laughed, pulling her close, kissing her ravenously.

Trust Me

Dear diary,
Sunday afternoon spent by the blanket box...
again. It seems like we live there! Not that I'm
complaining. I've been so tired lately that it's
been a relief to have somewhere peaceful to go
where I don't have to think about deadlines for
getting wedding dresses made. Pen asked me
to marry him, again. I looked him right in his
hopeful big blue eyes and said "Pen, nothing
would give me more pleasure than to walk
around Calico Bay, and to be called your wife.
I want to be Mrs Grille.'' He nearly fainted. I
know it was hard for him to broach the subject
again, but I'm so glad he did. He's the love of my
life, and it's time for our deep and abiding love
to be recognised publicly. And to be honest, I'm
sick of everyone calling him the town bachelor.
Bachelor, my foot! We've been wed to each other
in our hearts for most of our lives. We agreed
to keep it quiet till next week, and then we'll
hold a party at Bluey's Café and announce our
engagement. I'll tell Bluey before the party so she
gets a little warning!

Thursday morning...
I'm numb. This will break Pen's heart, but I have
to tell him. I have to tell him why I've changed
my mind. We can't get married.

Thursday night...
Pen and I went for a walk by Bendigo Creek.
I needed to know we wouldn't be overheard,
especially by Bluey. Especially in these early days.

I've never heard a grown man sob like he did tonight. "It can't be true!" he said, over and over.

This morning, Dr Baker confirmed my suspicions: I have leukaemia. "Six months, max", he said. Six months to say goodbye to the two loves of my life. Six months to fit in another lifetime. Six months.

Bluey sat on the bed crying. Clayton held her in his arms. There wasn't anything he could say to heal the hurt.

I haven't seen Pen all week. No visits, no phone calls. I drove around to check he was alright, but he'd locked himself in the shed and yelled out to me to "go away". He's not taking this well at all. I want to wrap my arms around him and tell him things will be okay, but I'd be lying. I'd finally said yes to him, and now I was not only saying no, I was saying goodbye. But now, more than ever, I need his love. I need him to hold me so I have the strength to tell Bluey.

Bluey had to stop reading. She was finding it hard to breathe. Not once had she considered what it must have been like for her mother to share the news that she was dying. Bluey had been so shaken, that all she could think of was her own life...a life without her mother. *An orphan all over again,* is what she'd thought at the time.

'I love our plans for the land, and the house, but I want to do more. We nearly lost it...it could have all turned to concrete, but now it has been given new life. I want to put most of that land into trust so that no one can ever develop on it,' Bluey said firmly. 'I'm going to see Hart tomorrow, and put it into action, but I need your help. I need you to walk through that entire piece of land, from Briar Ridge to Bendigo Creek to the secret spring and over to the tip of Calico Bay. I want every area assessed, recorded, and preserved.'

Clayton said, 'Slow down, honey, talk a little slower so I can keep up with you. You're like a Concorde jet! These ideas are brilliant, but you have to let me catch up.'

'Okay, I want the land where they're buried to definitely go into trust, and so too, the spring. We can keep the top field and Briar's Ridge in my name... *our* names', she smiled, sealing their future, 'and open it up for creating a market garden for the teenagers; and we can keep a few acres free near the café and put in picnic tables and maybe a barbecue area. What do you think?' she asked, trying to be mindful of slowing down.

'It's great. You know, I could make some wooden playground equipment, and put in a little park,' he suggested.

'Yes! Would you be able to manage the land?'

'I'd be honoured.'

She picked up the diary again, with a huge smile of satisfaction, feeling hopeful about the future: *their* future.

You are the love of my life, I told Pen. I said that if I could choose differently, I would have married him on the porch steps of our primary school. I didn't know how it would all turn out. But this, I know: that man has loved me stronger, harder, softer than any other man on Earth could have ever done. I wouldn't change that for the world.

Tears trickled down Bluey's cheeks, not for the first time. 'All I ever do these days is cry. Look at me!' she moaned.

'Your mum died a month ago, Bluey. You're going to be crying a lot more, with or without this diary stirring up feelings. But it doesn't matter how many tears you cry, because they'll never get rid of your beautiful smile. That smile was the reason I fell in love with you. The way your lips move and how the dimples crease your cheeks, and that your wide eyes light up like a Christmas tree at the slightest bit of joy. No amount of crying will ever change who you are,' he promised. 'For now, though, you really have to trust those tears. They're an important part of your journey.'

"Cat Got Your Tongue, Boy?"

When twenty-two-year-old Elsie Grille fell on the kitchen floor tiles and broke her top two front teeth, it wasn't the first time that Max Grille had put her there. But it was the first time a six-year-old boy had yelled at his father to stop. 'Leave my Mamma alone!' he called from his hiding place in the pantry. 'Stop making her cry!'

Dishevelled and smelling of tobacco and rum, Max Grille lunged towards Pen and pulled him to the kitchen sink.

'Got something to say?' he boomed into the terrified child's ear. 'Don't ever speak to me like that,' he slurred. 'You need your mouth washed out with soap.' Ruthlessly pulling the child's tongue out of his mouth, drunken Grille grabbed it in his filthy, grease-stained hands and used a scrubbing brush and soap to make his point: 'That'll teach you to speak when you're not spoken to!'

Pen gagged and choked, almost passing out.

Ironically, it was the half-empty rum bottle on the table, calling out to Max Grille to take another swig, which saved Pen from another bout with his old man. The drunken figure staggered from the kitchen: the hub of family life. This was Pen Grille's family: a terrified mother who was six-months pregnant, and a forty-year-old, out-of-work, drunken father.

Pen crawled on the floor beside his bleeding mother. She'd stopped crying now, and was curled up in a ball, shaking uncontrollably.

'I'm sorry,' Pen said. 'Mama, I'm sorry I didn't save you.' He wrapped his young arms around her, trying to soften the blow, nudging himself under the skirts of her dress for protection.

It wasn't the first time his mother was flattened to the ground, and it wasn't the last. But Pen had learnt his lesson: speak when you're spoken to.

Elsie died three weeks later, when 'Till Death Do Us Part' punched her one too many times.

Pen had dawdled home from school, never keen to be faced with the prospect of family war. It was Pen who found his mother's body splayed on the front steps, blood still dripping from her lifeless corpse.

Max Grille was charged with murder, and Pen never saw him again. He was taken in by his late mother's sister, Aunty Jean, and his maternal grandmother, Jessica Cotter. With only one friend, Hart, he floundered through childhood, barely uttering a word. Max Grille wouldn't be coming back. He'd never be able to scrub the poor boy's tongue again, but Pen didn't know that for sure.

Just What The Doctor Ordered

Dear diary...

Dr Baker has told Pen that he must do something about his high blood pressure: that he was a bomb just waiting to explode. Tick, tick, tick, he said. "I don't care what you do, Pen, old mate, but do something, please: drugs, meditation, herbs, hell, even homeopathy... just don't ignore this!" But Pen shrugged his shoulders and walked away, Doctor Baker confided in me later.

Pen has been under daily stress from some development company called Jackson-Briggs. They phone him every day and late into the night; they send letters, and they turn up uninvited on his doorstep. They want his land, all two-hundred acres of it. Pen thought it was a joke that they'd applied to the council for planning permission, several years before, and got it! It's not even their land, and yet they've got permission to build a massive development on there once it's acquired.

"Over my dead body," he grunted to me today. "They'll never get this property."

We picked out the spot today: the land where I'm going to be buried. It's a two-acre strip of scrub adjacent to Bendigo Creek. It was where Pen first whispered that he loved me. And I mean whispered! He was quieter than a church mouse. I wondered if he'd actually wanted me to hear. He has refused to let me buy the land, but has insisted that he'll get deeds drawn up in Bluey's name.

Bluey thought of the health of her mother and of Pen... both ticking time bombs, each in their own way. They were staring their mortality in the face, and making decisions neither of them wanted to make. In that moment, she picked up the phone, and made an appointment at Calico Bay Surgery to see Dr Baker.

The doctor talked with her for some time, doing all the routine examinations. 'Bluey, you're in great health. Really, you are. You're in the prime of your life. Enjoy every second of it. You're fertile; you're happy. Most people don't have this amount of joy in their lives when they lose a loved one, but you're positively glowing. Clayton Lansen has been good for you. He really has. If it's babies you're thinking of, then you should know that you're good to go,' he smiled. 'Pen and Emily would have loved Clayton. They really would have. It's a shame they didn't get to know him, but sometimes life works out in funny ways.'

There was a skip in her step as she walked out the front door, and headed back home to the arms of her lover.

The Tree House

'I want to show you something,' Bluey said to Clayton after breakfast on Sunday morning. He followed her outside, and up to the far end of the garden. As they stood under a huge pepperina tree, she said 'Pen built me this tree house. I've not been up there in years. I used to play in there all the time: often on my own, or with Olivia; it didn't matter. It was my secret place. My safe place. I want to go up there again and play. Will you come up there with me and teach me to play your guitar?' she asked, hoping that he'd agree.

'Of course I will, but I better check it's still safe!'

Clayton spent the next couple of hours surveying it for structural integrity. 'Pen was bloody amazing with wood,' was all Clayton had to say as they clambered up there with morning tea and a twenty-year-old guitar.

Along the window ledge, nestled between the yellow gingham curtains, were half-a-dozen rag dolls, all bleached from years of sunlight, and suffocating under thick, dust-laden cobwebs.

'Should have brought a duster,' Bluey laughed.

By the time they climbed down from the treehouse for lunch, there were blisters on Bluey's fingers.

'That really hurts. I had no idea that learning to play the guitar would be such hard work!'

'The best things in life often take effort, but you know, you grow to love those blisters. They toughen up, and they show you how far you've come.'

Clayton made some sandwiches for their lunch, and looked over his shoulder to find Bluey rummaging through an old sewing box that had belonged to her mother.

'I'm going to make some new curtains for the tree house,' she said out loud, but more to herself. 'You never know when someone might want to play up there.'

He knew exactly what she was thinking, and wondered just how many children she planned on having.

Afterwards, Clayton relaxed on the verandah, reading the Sunday paper, and Bluey headed to her bedroom to reread an old diary entry that her mother wrote when Bluey was seven years old.

Dear diary...
I overheard Bluey in the treehouse today. She was talking to her dolls and saying "I'm your mummy, and I'm going to love you just like my mummy loves me. I'll never leave you alone, and I will make you tasty food, and give you lots of cuddles. That's what mummies do."

My heart melted. This is what motherhood means to her: lots of love. It could have all been so different. She could have gone through childhood never knowing, never remembering, what it means to have someone love so powerfully that they'd protect you from anything; that they'd always fight your corner. I left her playing, and tiptoed across the grass. If there was anything I was ever worried about, it's all vanished now. I know she'll be okay.

Green Fingers

Bluey sipped fresh pineapple juice. The heat was sweltering, and she'd been at the café since before dawn. From mid-afternoon, she'd been interviewing teenagers. They arrived, hot and bothered, in their school uniforms, lugging heavy school bags onto the café verandah, as eager to get a part-time job as they were to get out of the scorching heat. There had been eight applicants in all, each desperate to find their way in the world. In the end, she decided they should all get a job. Bluey arranged for them to meet in the top field on Saturday afternoon.

She hadn't been to the old farmhouse all week, but had left Clayton to tidy up the garden. The house was now called *Mountain View Lodge*, but to Bluey's surprise, he'd done more than tidy up. He'd completely transformed the practical, rough-shod farmer's yard into a beautiful garden. There'd been trees planted, including a small orchard of apricots and mulberries to the side of the house. A large border of pretty perennials to the north would catch the morning Sun, and the vegetable beds had been weeded, and young seedlings planted. From the perimeter of the verandah, hanging basket after hanging basket of draping lobelia flowers adorned the house like a bride's blue garter.

Towards the dam, he'd built a couple of wooden benches.

Bluey stood, transfixed. 'You're a miracle worker,' she gasped.

'This was so much fun,' he replied. 'I've had such a great week here. Hey, what time do those kids arrive?'

'In about half an hour,' she said, looking up the back towards the top field. 'What have you done up there?' she asked, her eyes squinting in the sunlight.

'Re-fenced it,' he said proudly. 'I've also ordered some rolls of rabbit wire to keep those pesky things from eating all the veg. The hardware store is delivering me a bunch of gardening tools, too, so we can set up the vegetable planting as soon as you want. I'll build a small wooden shed, too, so we can keep the tools on site.'

'I can't believe how quickly everything's happening.'

The teenagers all arrived separately, and Bluey hoped their initial enthusiasm wouldn't wear off in a hurry. There was so much they could learn from Clayton, and from the land. Bluey was also keen to see if any of them wanted to learn to cook some of the produce, and had ideas about teaching cooking classes later in the year. Her thoughts turned to Sri Lanka, and she wondered whether they'd be too busy here to go off travelling.

A few hours later, Bluey said 'Let's get grandmother. I can't wait any longer!'

They found Maria Herring in the back garden, watering her orchids. 'Hello my dears,' she smiled as they walked towards her across the lawn. 'What a lovely surprise.'

Bluey kissed her on the cheek. 'We've got a surprise for you, actually. Have you got a spare couple of hours? There's something we'd like to show you,' Bluey said, trying to keep it a secret.

'Yes, of course. Let me just lock the door and get my bag.' Maria Herring was rather spritely for a woman in her late seventies. She'd kept herself fit by being an avid gardener, and taking long walks every day.

They drove back to Calico Bay, with Bluey talking a hundred miles an hour about all the projects happening with the teenagers, and about the woodturning. She filled her grandmother in about all sorts of things, including Clayton moving in with her, but she had to bite her tongue a few times so she could keep the house a surprise.

'Slow down, Bluey,' Clayton had to remind her every thirty seconds. 'You talk faster than you drive!'

'Oh my, this is a lovely house,' Maria said as they pulled off the dirt road into the driveway. 'Are we visiting someone?'

'Not exactly,' Bluey said, opening the car door for her grandmother, and taking her by the hand. 'Come inside.'

'In a moment dear, just let me enjoy this garden and that lovely mountain view. Whoever lives here really must love this place,' she said.

Bluey looked over to Clayton and smiled. He winked back at her.

'That's called Briar Ridge,' Clayton said, pointing up to the mountain.

'Granny, I own this place now, but I'm hoping, I'm really hoping, that you'll make this your home. I know it might seem remote, all alone on this dirt road at the back of the bush, but my house is only a kilometre away down that track.' And she started speaking at lightning speed again. 'Clayton's been here gardening and painting. He even made you a coffee table, and those benches down by the dam.'

Clayton squeezed Bluey's hand, and they both noticed the tears trickling down Maria's face.

'How incredibly thoughtful of you, my dear. I've lived at Saran Hill almost all of my life. Whatever possessed you to think I'd want to leave that behind and start again?'

Bluey's heart sank.

As she swayed with disappointment, she could feel Clayton catch her. After a few moments of silence, the old woman spoke again.

'I could think of nothing more perfect. Of course I'd love to live here,' she said, walking over to the dam. 'This place is really special.'

Maria Herring sat on a wooden bench, hand-carved by Clayton, and said 'I'd been wondering if I should move into a retirement home, you know, for a bit of company. But this? This is so much better.' She smiled. 'I could come down for a cup of tea at the café in the mornings, and take a little stroll on the bay,' she said to herself, but loud enough for them to hear. 'The sea air will do me good.'

'I could come and look after the gardens for you, do the weeding, mow the lawn...' Clayton offered.

'I'm not that old, young man,' she smiled. 'You can help me if you like, but I'm quite capable of pulling a few weeds if I set my mind to it.'

And in that moment, Bluey and Clayton knew exactly where Bluey got her determination from!

'I'll go inside and put the kettle on,' Clayton said, and left the women on their own for a few minutes.

'Come inside, Grandmother. You'll love it. There's so much character in that old house. And Clayton's done a beautiful job of redecorating it. If you don't like the colours, we can paint it all back to white again. And if you don't like the curtain fabric, I can change that to...'

'Hush, child, hush. Everything will be just fine.' For the first time, in a very long time, Maria Herring felt at peace with herself, and with the world, and with all the losses she'd endured over the years. Her granddaughter was back in her life, and they had a lot of catching up to do.

Two days later, Clayton and Reg drove the pick-up truck to Maria's home and began the long job of moving her life from one house to another. One life to another.

Maria stayed at Bluey's house overnight while everything was being transported.

A Picture Paints a Thousand Words

The face of the Moon was in a three-quarter position, ingressing to the sign of Scorpio: a time for revelations.

'Tell me about my mother, my *birth* mother…your daughter. I want to know everything about her. I never did before. I had a mother, you see. I had no need to know about a woman I'd never meet, but I do now. I *really* do. Please tell me,' begged Bluey as she sat on the sofa with her grandmother, sipping tea.

Maria Herring said 'I thought you'd never ask. Of course I want to tell you about her. She was my whole world…and so were you.'

'I had Marlene just shy of my sixteenth birthday. She was born out of wedlock, and we had a wedding when she was three weeks old. My father was surprisingly supportive. Things were different back then. It was quite an insult to wholesome living to have sex before marriage, let alone bring a baby into the world,' Maria said. Her eyes lit up as she remembered her youth.

'Wait here a minute,' she said, and went to the spare room and got a box out of her suitcase.

'Would you like to see photos of her as a baby?' Maria asked, not wanting to assume that Bluey would want a visual reminder of the woman she'd lost so young in her life.

'Oh yes!' Together they looked through a box of faded photographs. 'She looks like me when I was a little girl,' Bluey said, shocked by the resemblance.

'That's one of the main reasons I couldn't raise you my dear. It would have been like looking at my daughter every day. The pain would have been too intense.'

'I see that,' Bluey acknowledged, gently placing her hand on the wrinkled hands of her maternal grandmother. 'I really see that.'

'Marlene was a strong woman. She was quite feisty

in her way. Don't get me wrong. She was well liked, and had lots of lovely friends, but they all knew that she couldn't be walked over. When she became pregnant with you, something changed. I'd never seen her so calm and centred before. It was like she really understood that she was growing a baby, and that she was responsible for how she expressed her emotions. "That baby hears everything" she said to me when she was eight-months pregnant. She was such a fantastic mother to you, Bluey. She took you everywhere, and didn't believe in babysitters. Their plan was to move to the country and raise you away from the city.' Maria Herring sighed. 'But I look at your life now, and I know, for the first time since that terrible, fateful day, that everything has happened as it was meant to. Marlene brought you into this world and gave you the best three years of her life, and then Emily— soul-filled Emily—gave you the best years of her life. Do you know how blessed you are to have had two mothers love you like that?' A tear trickled down her jawline, and slipped onto her collar.

'Oh yes grandmother, I do.'

Dear diary...
Bluey's been looking after me every day. She looks exhausted. Despite her tan, she has a ghostly appearance. These past few months have battered her. The doctor says I'll have to move into the hospice soon. I won't be able to write much more. I'm too weak.

In the hospice...
It won't be long now. Pen comes here and sits with me all through the night, every single night, in the hard, old, plastic chair. You'd think the nurses could be a bit more accommodating.

He doesn't say much. Nothing new there. But he doesn't need to. He really doesn't. He's here, with me, and that's all that matters. I won't be able to write any more. The doctor says I haven't got long to go.

Hot and Spicy!

Reg Vardy delivered a box of sweet potatoes to the café, and said they were free. He'd never get them sold in time so she might as well put them to good use. "Reg the Veg", Olivia cheekily nicknamed him. He hung out on the verandah most afternoons, like a love-sick limpet; ginger freckles splattered across his face and neck inviting someone—anyone—to connect the dots.

'Can you use them?' he asked Bluey, leaning against a post on the verandah, at 6.45 that morning. His jeans were always too tight, and about three inches too short. Bluey, however, was able to see beyond the overgrown teenager.

'You betcha,' Bluey smiled, always keen to have a surplus of any vegetable that was on offer. They'd been friends since primary school, and Reg made no secret of having a soft spot for her. His biggest regret was marrying Margaret Shaw at eighteen. He'd been regretting it for the past ten years, and as each year passed and Bluey remained single, he regretted it even more. Six children later, and he still hoped that one day Bluey would *see* him.

He left her to the laugh of the morning kookaburra perched on the bottlebrush tree, and she continued with her preparations.

Dividing up a large bunch of dark-pink gerberas, Bluey placed a vase on each table of the verandah.

Afterwards, she rummaged around the box of CDs, finally settling on an old Al Martino one that had belonged to her mother. The crooner's soft tones filled the empty café, and Bluey turned it up so she could hear him from the kitchen. She thrived on the early morning solitude before Olivia and the customers came into the café. This was her private time, and her time for being creative.

'Now, sweet potatoes. What shall I do with you guys?' she mused, getting out her oak chopping board and paring knife.

Flicking through her vast collection of hand-written recipes, she found herself once again under the turquoise skies of the East African coast. All at once, she was twenty-three years old, and having the time of her life. *Sweet potatoes and spicy-peanut sauce*, that's what she'd make today. Back then, she'd eaten them under starry skies: the handsome Afrikaan, Carl Hagen, licking the hot sauce off her fingers as they sat around a crackling fire on an isolated beach late one evening.

Bluey had just finished three weeks of volunteering in a small orphanage for children whose parents had died of AIDS, and spent her final week on African soil learning to cook local food.

Carl was the son of her host family, and they were instantly attracted to each other. By day, she laughed as they ran, hand in hand, up sand dunes; and together they swam naked in a lake, like honeymooners. Her room was a lodge in the wilderness, built on stilts; but she didn't sleep alone. Carl made sure of that. It was the briefest of affairs: begun on the day they met, and ending just as quickly a week later, on the day she flew back to Australia. Passionate, intense and invigorating, but she knew it was lust, not love. There was no risk of heartbreak with Carl Hagen.

Bluey mixed together spices: cinnamon, cayenne, cardamom, ginger, and mashed them with plump sweetcorn kernels and cooked sweet potato.

Carl Hagen was her passport to exploring sexuality in a way that was new. It was her first pleasurable intensely intimate experience, and it allowed her to know that she did have a future where she could enjoy her body, and not feel ashamed, degraded or victimised. She continued to reminisce. Carl's gentle touch had shown her that she didn't have to be afraid. He discovered the woman in her who was aching to be freed from captivity, and she marvelled at the pleasure which coursed through her blood.

Africa was a continent of contrasts, and as she prepared a rocket and orange salad, she recognised that she'd left a little of her soul beneath one of its spectacular sunsets. She saw the contrast within herself: unfathomable grief for the mother and surrogate father who wouldn't be coming back, and subterranean love for the man who wouldn't be leaving.

Later, she mixed a ginger drink according to East African tradition: fresh ginger root, limes, cloves and oranges; and her heart came alive to the memory of donkeys pulling carts down narrow dirt roads, and her and Carl dancing to drums, marimba and xylophone by the village bonfire. They'd spent the day exploring the markets: a parade of brilliant colours, busy with activity and exotic foods. It was here, in Thabo market, as she ate guavas, that she discovered the time-old skill of improvised cooking based on the foods which were local, as well as taking into account the preference of the guests who'd be dining.

She closed her eyes and remembered how they ran through an intense thunderstorm as Carl looked for shelter. He took her down what the locals knew as *Lovers' Lane*: a road shrouded by oleander, bougainvillea and hibiscus. They made love in the tempestuous rain, and Bluey had never felt more alive and womanly in all her life. Steam rose off their bodies as the turbulent raindrops fell onto their burning-with-desire skin. Everything about that hot and spicy week in the arms of Carl Hagen went into her chalkboard menu that day.

Chickpea and coriander soup
Sweet-potato patties with spicy-peanut sauce
Bananas fried in coconut oil with lime & coconut ice cream
Ginger drink

A dozen glass Mason jars lined the wooden kitchen window sill, each filled with a bunch of fresh herbs. As

Bluey cut a handful of coriander leaves, she recalled Carl's description of coriander's origins, and how it had been used since biblical times. He'd filled her head with so many legends and stories about herbs and spices that she vowed one day to write a book on her travels. *Coriander is a chameleon*, he said, kissing her and lingering near the nape of her neck. It could spice just about everything in the kitchen.

Coriander is like a woman, he laughed out loud. *Its flavours can't be controlled. You're taken in by the sensual musk*, he said, kissing her sweetly, *the raw, earthy scent of thyme and citrus. Before you know it, you're under her spell.* Bluey's body was pulsing to his tantalising touch. Coriander-lesson learned!

Carl Hagen demonstrated how to grind and toast the coriander seeds, and how floral the whole seeds could be. They could be both nutty and taste of curry. The fresh leaves were shaped like parsley, and hinted of citrus.

Using a mix of fresh and dried coriander, she left her soup to simmer on the stove top.

Picking out a Michael Bublé CD, Bluey found the track, *Sway*.

> *When marimba rhythms start to play*
> *Dance with me, make me sway*
> *Like a lazy ocean hugs the shore*
> *Hold me close, sway me more*

Bluey placed one hand on her belly, and swayed her hips from side to side like a palm tree in the ocean breeze. She felt good, but she was no longer thinking of Carl Hagen. No. Her hips were swaying to thoughts of a new man: Clayton Lansen.

Never Too Late

Clayton came in through the back kitchen door of Bluey's Café with a smile on his face. 'What are you so happy about?' Bluey asked, catching more than a hint of his joy. She carefully placed a tray of honey and macadamia muffins into the hot oven.

'Your grandmother! Every time I drive up to the top field, she has another gentleman visitor on her verandah. And today there are four men on her verandah having morning tea!'

'I think she's a bit old for a chaperone, Clayton,' Bluey admonished, and smiled at the thought. 'Well, at least she's not alone. I wasn't entirely sure if the location would suit her, being away from other houses; but hey, if she's got gentlemen callers then that can only be a good thing, right?' Bluey gazed over at him, and battered her eyelashes. She knew exactly what Clayton was thinking.

'Please don't tell me you think that people stop having a sex life because they're in their seventies or eighties?'

'I just never saw your grandmother that way before.' He blushed a little. 'I thought she'd be up there knitting or something. Isn't that what elderly women do?'

Bluey walked over to him, hands on hips, then leaned over and kissed him slowly, deeply, tauntingly. 'Not us Herring women, apparently,' she laughed: every cell in her body overjoyed to be reconnected to her biological maternal ancestry. 'I'll be kissing you like this when I'm 30, 40, 50, 60, 70, 80...and every year in between. Once a woman, always a woman,' she said, and went to wash a cucumber. 'Don't ever forget that, Mr Lansen. We're red-blooded!'

'Come back here!' he smiled, wrapping his tanned arms around her curved waist. 'And I'll be kissing you right back, just like this.' She found her knees going wobbly, butterflies flying in her tummy.

'Do you think we should tell her about the blanket box by the spring?' he whispered into her ear.

'No!!!!! That's our place now!' Bluey insisted. 'She can find her own lovers' nest!' And then, they both doubled over with laughter.

On Saturday morning, when Maria Herring joined Alfie Dennis for brunch on the verandah of Bluey's Café, her granddaughter suggested that she might like to have a psychic reading with Serena. 'Why not?' Bluey smiled. 'It's not like you don't have a future.' She winked in Alfie's direction.

Maria Herring was a spritely 76-year-old, and had a lot of miles still to register on the clock. Her bobbed silver hair swung around her square jawline, highlighting her high cheekbones. She rose to the challenge: 'Book me in!'

Later, she took her seat in the velvet-surround booth, and listened as Serena read the cards.

'I see you knitting,' she started, but was quickly interrupted by an indignant Maria Herring.

'Every grey-haired woman knits!' she said. 'Tell me something a little less predictable.'

Taken aback, Serena responded. 'Yes, but you'll be knitting baby booties. You've never done that before.'

Maria Herring sat back in the chair. It was true, she'd never knitted baby booties before.

'There is love around you. I see invitations. Wedding invitations.'

Maria Herring's heart set aflutter. Was Alfie that serious about her? They'd made love a few times, after their weekly reading group, but she'd only seen him as a pleasurable companion, not as a permanent fixture.

'Go on,' she insisted, suddenly keen to know more.

Bluey's ears were stretching around the door of the kitchen and past the coffee machine. 'Oh my god!' she whispered to Olivia, both giggling into their hands like naughty school girls as the revelations began.

The Old Rainwater Tank

The rain had been long overdue, and when it began falling on the tin roof late that night, Bluey and Clayton sighed with relief. It began lightly, so lightly they wondered if they were imagining the sporadic spatter of raindrops. And then it came down, each spit pounding furiously and sounding like a truckload of coconuts being dropped from on high.

'About bloody time,' he muttered. 'That rainwater tank at Maria's needs replacing; it's got a lot of rust at the bottom, and I should put up a windmill, too. That'll be next on my list. Just a shame I didn't get around to it before the rain,' Clayton said, snuggling in closer to Bluey as they looked at each other in bed.

'You never stop, do you?' she smiled. 'Just one job after another…'

'Gotta make myself useful; earn my keep,' Clayton laughed. But they both knew he didn't have to earn anything. They were in this together: partners.

That darned rainwater tank! Why did he have to mention that? It pulled her thoughts to when she was 22 years old. She didn't want to go back there, ever. But memories have a way of dragging you to the rear-view mirror, when you should be looking in front of you: pulling you backwards, when you least expect it.

Keith Kunner had been asking her out on a date for four months. She'd said no, absolutely not. Keith had sex with every young woman in a twenty-kilometre radius. There was no way she was getting involved with him! After her experience with Roger, she was so wary of being hurt, physically and emotionally. Olivia warned her not to go near him. 'He's trouble, Blue. Stay away,' she said seriously.

Bluey had dated Zed Kaller for the five months

previous, but they'd never done more than peck each other on the cheek at the end of each night. Finally, the young shearer decided to move to the Northern Territory to work on a sheep station. He'd begged Bluey to move up with him. 'You could cook for the shearers,' he said.

'Mutton stew? I don't think so!' And they parted ways gently.

But Keith Kunner, he was not so gentle. And he was determined to get Bluey Miller as a notch on his conquest belt. 'Just one date,' he insisted, straddling a chair on the verandah outside her café late one Friday afternoon. 'And if you have such an awful time, we'll never go out again. I promise,' he smiled; but she didn't entirely trust him. Her gut instinct said: *Don't go near him.* Her mother said 'You can't be serious.' And Pen said 'You'll live to regret it.'

Despite the warnings, Bluey succumbed, and by Friday night she was on the back of his motor bike riding up to the Helston Gap. At the top, they got off the bike, put their helmets on the ground, and sat at the side of the road. He lit up a fag, and took a drag.

'So, Roger told me all about you,' he said in a way that made her pulse shoot through her skin like a rabbit darting from gunshots. She rapidly regretted her decision to go out with him.

'Roger lied,' she insisted. 'I'm a virgin. I've never had sex with anyone, and Keith Kunner I am *not* about to have sex with you,' she said firmly, looking him right in the eye. 'I'm never going to have sex with you! Take me home!'

But he didn't take her home. He dragged her, kicking, screaming and fighting, up into the dense scrubby bush away from the roadside. 'Don't fight me,' he snapped, pulling at her hair. 'You want this as much as I do,' Keith growled into her ear. She was gagging from the smell of his garlic-and-beer breath. With one hand, he pulled up her T-shirt, brutally groping her breast. His teeth sunk into her other one so violently that he drew blood from her nipple. She could see it on his teeth when he looked up at her and grinned. Bluey turned her face away.

With his other hand, he pulled down her jeans and forced her to the ground.

'I don't want this. I really don't!' she sobbed, wiping the dripping mucus from her nose onto her bare arms, but he took no notice of her plea, and pinned her arms down by her side.

Should she fight him with all her strength and risk what happened to her on the night of her eighteenth birthday with Roger? In a split second, she decided against it. There was no point screaming. No one would hear her. Bluey lay still. She didn't fight. She didn't protest. Instead, she shut her eyes, gritted her teeth, and barely breathed.

'Good girl, I knew you wanted it!' he snickered, as he forced his rock-hard shaft into her, severing her like a spear; shunting it back and forward like a farmer knocking a post into untamed ground: relentless, repetitive; finally spilling his poison into the soft folds of her warm, tender flesh. Keith Kunner didn't say a word. Bluey's focus wavered between his painful pounding, and the discomfort of the gumnuts digging into her bare bottom. He stopped a minute later, when he felt relief; a momentary grunt of pleasure escaping his stained yellow teeth. If this was sex, Bluey didn't like it. The whole ordeal had hardly lasted a couple of minutes, but to Bluey, it felt like hours, and the memory would last a lifetime. It was a nightmare that she'd never wake up from.

Keith Kunner stood up to his full height, zipped up his black jeans, snickered, then said: 'Good girl. Roger was right! You are an easy lay.' He spat on the ground, and laughed. 'Slut!' Another notch gained. He got on his bike, and left her alone: bare chested, and semen dripping down her legs, as she sobbed softly into the black soil.

A little while later, when it was apparent that he

wasn't coming back for her, she got dressed, and walked through the bush, until she reached the outskirts of Pen's land. Keith Kunner was gone, but the stench of his sweat clung to her skin and lingered in her nostrils. She needed water. Bluey was desperate to wash herself.

Pen wasn't home; she knew that because his white utility truck wasn't parked in the driveway. She found herself sitting underneath his old rainwater tank, crying her heart out. Why were men so unkind? Why did men think they could just take what they wanted? *I'm a nice person*, she told herself, over and over again. *Why do I attract such rotten men?* She turned on the tap at the bottom of the tank, and washed herself clean, wincing each time her trembling touch met upon tender and bruised places.

Bluey used her fingernails to scrub her underpants, and then rinsed them with rainwater. Hung to dry on a rusty nail alongside her jeans and T-shirt, she sat back and shivered: with cold, and with fear; with the certain knowledge that her life would never be the same again.

'Hey, what's going on?' Pen asked, when he found her out there the next morning, still crying, and half naked.

'Nothing,' she lied, but Pen had known her most of her life. He knew that things were far from fine. Twenty-two-year-old women didn't sit under rainwater tanks crying. He knew exactly what that mongrel had done, and Pen was not going to let him get away with destroying his girl's life.

'Your mother is beside herself with worry. Where have you been? Have you slept here all night?'

Pen took her hand, and said 'Come with me.' He went inside and got his terry-towelling dressing gown to wrap around her. Pen didn't say a word in the car, and Bluey was surprised when he didn't drive her home. Instead, he drove to Dr Baker's house. It was a Saturday morning, and his clinic would be shut. 'Jeb,' he said to his old mate, choking on the words. 'I need you to give her a check up. I need you to tell me she's okay,' and wiping a tear from his eye, Pen went and sat in the car and waited. He waited, and waited and waited.

Dr Jebediah Baker made a strong brew of tea, and sat her down. He didn't examine her for at least two hours, but encouraged her to talk. Eventually, she did. She told him not just about Keith but also about Roger, and how her mother had mended her. He shook his head from side to side.

'I'm so sorry Bluey. Not all men are like this. I'm sorry that you've had such bad experiences. Promise me that you won't go out with men like this again,' he said kindly. 'Keith has had sex with so many women around here, and I hate to say this, but it's not the first time I've had a woman come to me because of him. He should be locked up! No, he should be shot,' the old doctor fumed, and kicked the table leg in anger.

He cleaned up her vulva with care and respect, checking the damage, and giving her antibiotics for the tears to her tender flesh.

Bluey sensed he'd done this job many times, and tilted her head to one side in shame.

'You are not the guilty party here, Bluey. This is not your fault!' He offered for her to use his shower. 'No one ever presses charges against Keith, and I imagine you're not going to either. But if you change your mind, I'll support you one hundred per cent,' he promised her. 'I'd like you to come to the surgery so I can do some tests for sexually transmitted diseases. Please don't let it make you feel disgusted or ashamed. It's just routine, really,' he promised. But a few weeks later, when the results came back that she'd contracted chlamydia, it no longer felt routine.

'These antibiotics will clear it up,' he said, trying to assure her when she leant forward and sobbed. 'Unfortunately, it's one of those silent diseases which can be pretty hard to detect as it doesn't show symptoms. If Pen Grille didn't bring you to me when he did; if you'd not told anyone, then I'm afraid you'd almost certainly become infertile. He did you a huge favour, in more ways than one.' Dr Baker made it clear that she'd had a lucky escape.

Bluey walked outside into the pouring rain. She turned back to look at the Doctor's Surgery, and thought how ironic it was that she'd grown up as such a healthy child. *I am never getting married*, she vowed as she left. *I hate men!*

It was some time before she saw Keith Kunner again. He had disappeared from Calico Bay as quickly as Roger had. She often wondered if he'd gone to Western Australia too. For quite a long time she was nervous about being at work alone. Each morning she would triple-check the doors were locked behind her. Karma would eventually catch up with Keith Kunner.

Three months later, Evert Franks proposed to Bluey on the verandah of the café. Neither Emily nor Pen objected to Evert, but they didn't warm to him either.

'He's kind, Mum,' Bluey had said one day. 'And he's gentle with me. He's never forced himself,' she said, confessing that they'd almost had sex in his father's hayshed, but that she wasn't ready to go that far. The experience had been rather different, but it wasn't something she thought she wanted to do with Evert Franks for the rest of her life.

She broke his heart at the same time as proffering a basket of peach muffins. 'I'm sorry, Evert, but we're just not made for each other. You're a good man. There'll be someone for you, I'm sure,' she promised; and six weeks later was standing in Abbot's Chapel watching him exchange vows with Dolly Templeton. 'Fickle, not?' Bluey whispered to Olivia as they stood there in their best dresses, red lipstick and three-inch heels, trying not to giggle.

Bluey sighed deeply, and wrapped her arms around Clayton's warm body, feeling his soft skin against her cheek. One day she'd tell him about the men in her past: good and bad; but not tonight. Tonight she just wanted to listen to the rain. Yes, listen to the rain, and feel safe next to a *good* man. Clayton was right: it was time for a new rainwater tank.

Snake Skin

Bluey took a stroll down by Bendigo Creek to visit the burial site of Emily and Pen, and lay down some flowers. She dug a small hole, and planted a bottlebrush bush. It would enjoy the shady area, and she could easily bring water over from the nearby creek if there were prolonged periods without rain.

Bottlebrush had been an easy choice for a memorial plant. Her mother had loved the one in front of the café, and often brushed her fingers against the crimson-red flowers with its pollen-coated ends. But it had been Bluey's memory of something she'd learnt on a course about Australian Bushflower Essences that made her choose this plant. It was prescribed for people going through major life changes. To Bluey, it seemed a perfect symbol. The flowers would come out in Spring, and again in Summer and Autumn.

After a while, she lit a small fire, surrounded by rocks so there was no risking of it spreading, and prepared to cook damper.

Pen had often brought her into the bush to enjoy some Aussie campfire bread, and was the first person to teach her to cook bread in this way. His recipe was simple:

2 cups self-raising flour
½ teaspoon salt
1 to 1½ cups milk
2 teaspoons sugar
2 teaspoons olive oil

He'd mix the flour, sugar and salt, then add the oil, finally adding milk or water, and mixed until it formed a soft dough. Pen would then knead it until smooth, and shape it around a clean stick. And for about twenty minutes, the pair of them would sit patiently while it cooked. Pen told her the name damper came about because of the need to damp the fire down before cooking the bread over the hot coals. All the men of the Outback could make damper: the easiest bread of all. The drovers could carry the dry ingredients, and they only needed to find a creek to add the water. If they didn't have water, they almost certainly had beer!

Bluey opened her backpack, and pulled out a container with dough she'd made at home. Gathering a scoop, she spread it onto the stick she'd whittled, and secured it on: an eight-inch-long doughy sock. Turning it slowly over the coals, she watched it turn from raw flour and water into cooked unleavened bread. When it had baked to perfection, she gently slid it off the stick, and drizzled some maple syrup inside. One day she'd bring Clayton here to enjoy damper, but for now, she wanted to be on her own and commune with the spirits of Pen and Emily.

Bluey sat on the ground watching the embers for the longest time, quietly chatting to Pen and Emily as if it was the most natural thing in the world.

Listening to the birds, and swiping the ants off her legs, she noticed a snake skin just a metre or so away from her. She wondered about the snake which had once inhabited it, and marvelled at how they outgrow skins and develop new ones. And then, an old memory came to the surface, bubbling up like water from a spring, nourishing her parched soul.

She'd been about 13 years old, just taking her first steps into the mysterious and overwhelming world of puberty. Bluey had been helping Pen clear some scrubland by the creek, and burning off old wood, when they came across a snake skin.

He'd patiently explained to Bluey that while young snakes shed their skins every few weeks, the adult snake does so only a few times a year. He told her that if she ever saw a snake skin, she could think of it as like a totem animal.

'It means there's a spiritual awakening taking place,' he'd said, mindful of the fact that Emily had let slip that Bluey's first menstrual period had arrived, and she was feeling awkward and insecure about her changing body and unpredictable emotions. No longer a child, but not yet a woman, either.

She couldn't help but smile to herself as she recalled how she first learnt about periods. They'd been up at the top field checking on Pen's horses, when Bluey noticed a long stringy rope of blood hanging from the mare's bottom.

'She's hurt,' Bluey whimpered that day.

'No, she's fine,' Pen replied calmly. 'She's got her period. It happens to all female mammals. One day, it will happen to you,' he said. 'It won't hurt,' he promised.

Pen told her that when a snake skin is your totem, you can expect to undergo a death—a symbolic death—and that when that happened, something new would be born. 'You have to leave the old self behind,' he'd said softly, 'so the new you can come through.'

She laughed at the difference between her mother's talk about the birds and the bees, and Pen's talk about snakes. Completely different approaches, but both so nurturing and caring of her development.

Bluey picked up the fragile skin and recognised that she too had been shedding her skin to make way for the new self which was emerging. A thought occurred to her. Once, she'd read about the snake as a symbol for her star sign, Scorpio. Apparently those born under this much-feared sign were here to experience a pivotal lifetime in the theory of reincarnation. Psychic Serena said it indicated that they'd have the gift of psychic awareness, intuition and a busy dream life.

She wondered about her link to the Underworld, and how she often received snippets of information from out of nowhere in the most uncanny way.

Biblically, the serpent was considered more subtle

than beasts of the field: elusive and rare. In her yoga class, Bluey had learnt about the subtle power of the kundalini rising up the spine. She laughed at the Christian idea of the *bad bad bad* snake of the Garden of Eden, doomed to crawl on its belly and eat dirt till the end of eternity. She felt there was something greater to this creature. It could transform itself: leave its skin behind.

'Scorpio,' she said out loud. 'Deeply emotional, highly sensitive and loyal. Yeah, that sums me up.' Bluey thought about Serena's description of the scorpion: a creature which can survive intense amounts of radiation; amounts that would kill most living creatures. Serena told her that the scorpion can survive being frozen, and it can hold its breath for three days. 'Don't underestimate your power,' she told her. 'You can survive anything.'

Thinking about the death of her birth parents, and then the deaths of Emily and Pen, she wondered how all four deaths had transformed her. As she recalled Pen's words about the snake shedding its skin, she realised that she had undergone a major psychological shedding.

Carefully picking up the old snake skin, she carried it home as her totem of transformation. On her walk back, Bluey thought about Scorpio as the only zodiac sign to have three animal totems: scorpion, snake and eagle. The latter totem was for perspective; the ability to rise above circumstances. She wondered if she could do that, too.

View from the Verandah

When Nettie Ford stopped by at closing time on Friday afternoon for her weekly order of a basket of banana muffins, she'd caught Bluey weeping to her mother's favourite song on the CD. It was Al Martino crooning *I'll Never Find Another You.*

> *There's a new world somewhere*
> *They call The Promised Land*
> *And I'll be there some day*
> *If you will hold my hand*
> *I still need you there beside me*
> *No matter what I do*
> *For I know I'll never find another you*

'My dear, it's been nearly five months now, it's time to move on. Your mother's not coming back,' she shook her head from side to side as she clutched the basket from Bluey's hands. 'Emily wouldn't want you moping around.' As she scuttled out of the café, her ample bottom wiggled beneath her yellow polka-dot skirt. If she hadn't moved off so swiftly, Bluey would have chased her out with the broom that was now in her hands.

She wanted to scream, but instead she turned up the CD, lined up the song again, and sang at the top of her voice.

The verandah had wrapped around three sides of the original Cotter House, but when Pen and his workmates renovated the building in preparation for the café, he converted the two side verandahs in order to extend interior space for the diners and to make a large walk-in pantry.

At the front of the sky-blue café, the verandah could comfortably fit in five tables, and seating for about 14 people. The red corrugated-tin roof fed water into three rainwater tanks, which Bluey used to keep the gardens around the café lush and green. A four-metre-high crimson bottlebrush bush grew near the steps leading up to the verandah, providing a burst of vibrant colour in Spring, Summer and Autumn. It was the favoured perch for two kookaburras. They were distinctive by the pale-blue colouring on their otherwise brown wings. Bluey often thought they matched the front of the café rather well.

Hanging off the café was a large six-feet-long slice of roughly cut timber, with the words *Bluey's Café* burnt into it. There was no way anyone would drive past that building: colourful, attractive, inviting and unique.

Large ferns thrived in old wooden barrels; a mixture of bird's-nest ferns and rough tree ferns, which brought a sense of coolness to the shady dining area. On each table there was a small white Moroccan-style lantern for holding tealight candles, and a bunch of hibiscus flowers. To the back of the café were several vegetable beds, and dozens of terracotta pots filled with salad leaves: spinach, chard, beet, mizuna, rocket. Nasturtiums rampaged across everything they could find. Bluey didn't mind. She loved to toss the flowers into salads for a burst of surprising colour.

When Clayton arrived ten minutes later, they sat on the verandah sipping fresh orange, passionfruit and mango nectar. It had been four-and-a-half months since the day he first stood there taking in the view of the bay, and had been awestruck by the sight of the beautiful woman who stood before him.

Bluey told him about Nettie and about the song she'd been singing, and how fed up she was of the expectation of some of the older people to 'just get on with it', as if enough time had passed. They also talked about Emily Miller, and her last months on Earth.

'She'd been tired for a while, and kept complaining of not being able to get rid of her cold. I didn't take too much notice at the time. Mum had a tendency to burn the candle at both ends, so I thought she just needed a good sleep.'

'She didn't think to have a check-up with the doctor?' Clayton asked.

'No, not at that stage. She finally went when the headaches came, and the vomiting started. It was only when she puked up over there on the beach, on a day that Dr Baker happened to be sitting in this very chair, that she took it seriously. He witnessed it, and wasn't taking no for an answer. But even after the blood tests came back, it was about another month before she finally told me.'

'That must have been hard,' Clayton said, holding her hand.

'It didn't sink in, really. I just thought with all the modern advances in medicine that she'd go into remission and life would carry on. But her immune system was too far gone for any chance of recovery.'

They were silent for several minutes, when Bluey recalled her mother's dying hours. 'Mum kept calling out "Mama" and turning her head towards the window. The nurse said it's common for a dying person to do that... that their vision has decreased so they're instinctively looking for the light. What a load of garbage! My mother had seen her deceased mother in those last hours. She'd seen the Light.'

Clayton sighed with empathy.

'In hindsight, are you glad you had the chance to say goodbye?' he asked.

'Yeah, I am. I'm sorry, though, that she suffered so much, especially in the last couple of weeks. It was truly awful to see her body so ravaged; her long, beautiful, shiny, brown hair all but gone.'

They continued to talk of death and dying, and Clayton eventually confided that his twin sister had drowned on a school camping trip, twenty five years ago. She was just ten years old.

'All this time together, and you've never told me this.

Why?' she asked, saddened both by the immense loss and also that he'd kept it to himself.

'I didn't want to take away from your grief. People often say "I know exactly how you feel", but no one can ever know how you feel, even if their loved one died from the exact same cause. I'm sorry. I wasn't deliberately trying to hide it from you. I promise,' Clayton said solemnly, then paused, and sighed deeply. 'It was hard enough that Janelle died, but it was made all the worse by the stupid things people say when you're grieving. They think they're helping you, but actually they're making the pain worse!'

Bluey could see he was reliving his sister's death all over again.

'You mean like "Stop crying; you're only making it harder for yourself" and other silly advice?' she said, remembering what Mrs Hetherington from the hairdresser had said on the morning of Emily Miller's funeral. 'Oh, and my all-time favourite: "At least she's not suffering any more", as if somehow this is supposed to make me feel better? Didn't they know I'd just lost my mother? Oh, and don't get me started on the feeble minister from Warrigo Chapel: "God never gives us more than we can handle". Well, frankly, God must have forgotten that when he took my mother!' Bluey spat into the air, remembering the unhelpful comments.

Clayton continued: 'The one we heard over and over was "God must have wanted her"…as if that somehow made our loss special. It was enough to make me want to become an atheist. All people ever need to say is "I'm so sorry for your loss". It's short, and to the point, and if it comes from the heart there's nothing else that needs to be said.'

Bluey nodded. She'd remembered how kind Olivia had been, and how she had acknowledged her pain, and promised her that she was there, night or day, no matter what. 'I'm not religious, but it's comforting when people say that they're holding you in their prayers, and in their thoughts.'

'What really helped me through losing Janelle was hearing so many of her school friends share about what a lovely person she was, and all the things they'd miss about her. Some of them, especially the boys, admitted that they didn't know what to say, but that sure felt more honest than the people who said thoughtless things. Her art teacher, Sally Striver, was the best,' Clayton smiled. 'She really seemed to get it, you know. For months and months afterwards, she'd ask how I was feeling. I could tell that it was something she really meant, and that nothing was more important to her than knowing I was okay. She single-handedly got me through the first year of Janelle's death.'

The day turned to night, and Bluey lit some lanterns. Clayton grabbed his guitar from the jeep, and he sang soft ballads as a slip of Moon rose over the shoreline. He finished off Emily Miller's favourite song, but when Bluey heard it she knew the words Clayton Lansen sang were for her; all for her.

There is always someone
For each of us they say
And you'll be my someone
For ever and a day
I could search the whole world over
Until my life is through
But I know I'll never find another you

With tears in her eyes, Bluey went and sat on Clayton's lap, and wrapped her arms around him. And in that moment, she prayed that God would never want to take him away from her; that Clayton wasn't 'special' enough for God to want him more than she did.

The Woodturner

Clayton stood in Pen Grille's old woodturning shed, by the large window overlooking the dam and scrubland, and smiled at his good turn of fortune. He'd grown to adore this space. As he took in the view before him, he reflected on how it had been life's misfortunes that had originally brought him to a woodturner's door. After the death of his sister, Clayton couldn't focus on school, and his work there just kept on deteriorating. Life felt meaningless, and he stumbled along through the years ahead.

At sixteen, he was visiting an old uncle for the weekend when he was introduced to a neighbour who turned wood for a trade. Clayton found it fascinating to watch him at work, and how he effortlessly turned a piece of rough wood into something which could be used. The kind man let him play with the tools of the trade, and Clayton soon discovered that not only did he have a flair for handling wood, but that woodturning was a lot of fun.

For his seventeenth birthday, Clayton's father bought him a lathe, gouge, beading tool, parting tool, chisel, scraper and an axe. He became an expert at turning any piece of wood into something magical.

At nineteen, he holidayed in Tasmania, and came across the beautiful land south-west of Hobart: a place where explorers discovered ancient tree trunks buried in the mud. The wood had been preserved, and this discovery led to Huon pine becoming known worldwide as the best timber for boating. Clayton developed a passion for sourcing the salvaged Huon pine, and by twenty two was working as a forest warden protecting vast swathes of native land. His passion for the trees around him, and his understanding of the natural ecology, soon found him in a courtroom fighting to save a farmer's land from certain destruction. Word quickly got out amongst other forest wardens when feature articles hit all of the Australian national newspapers. Clayton became known in certain circles as The Tree Whisperer. He also had an innate ability to see both sides of an argument, and to find mutually convenient and supportive resolution.

At the age of twenty seven, he was employed to represent a Nature Reserve in its battle against a large mining corporation on the Darling Downs in Queensland.

Meeting Saskia Spicato, a feisty Italian working on a vineyard in Stanthorpe, lured him back to the Sunshine State. Their tempestuous relationship lasted five years, amazingly, before she left him, broken-hearted but relieved, for an Argentinean billionaire. Clayton was grateful they'd parted ways, as he found the relationship utterly stressful, but whenever he'd tried to end it she would grab a kitchen knife and make him promise to stay.

As he stood surveying the delivery of salvaged Huon pine from his mate, Franko, his thoughts turned to Tasmania, and he sighed as he recalled that it was one of the most beautiful and pristine areas left of natural ecology anywhere on Earth.

Franko was always on the lookout for wood for him, and Clayton couldn't believe his luck.

He ran his hands over the grey-brown bark, and admired the length of the logs; some were more than forty-feet long. He loved the dense grain and close-spaced rings of Huon, a result of it being such a slow-growing tree. One of the oldest in Australia, some have been growing for three-thousand years. Clayton loved that it was such an easy timber to work with, and that it was virtually rot-proof because of its unique oil: methyl euganol. This essential oil gave it the distinctive smell that he loved so much: buttery, fragrant, sweet, woody, cedar-spice. He often used the oil as an aftershave. More than anything, he was captivated every time by the beautiful golden colour of the timber. Woodturning was fairly quick, and Clayton was prolific in his output. It was late on a Monday afternoon when he surprised Bluey in the back of the café. She was tidying up the afternoon's dishes.

'Close your eyes,' he whispered, when he crept up behind her. 'Keep them closed until I say you can open them.'

'Clayton Lansen, what are you up to?' she smiled. She'd grown to love his little surprises: picnics on the beach at midnight, day trips on a Sunday up to the mountains, singing her a song he'd just written, or lunch on a sailing boat, breakfast in bed, rose petals sprinkled on bed sheets. What was he up to now?

She heard him leave and come into the kitchen a few times, putting something on the bench, and heading back out to the jeep again.

'Okay, you can open them!' he smiled. 'Surprise!'

Bluey opened the cardboard boxes, and pulled out rolling pins, salt-and-pepper shakers, spoons and bowls, English lemon juicers and breadboards. Clayton had hand-crafted all of them from Huon pine.

'Do you like them?' he asked.

'Clayton, they're incredible. I can't believe that you've made these.' She found herself lost for words.

'They're not all for you, of course. I thought you could sell the spare ones in the café, if you like?'

'If I like? Of course I like!' She hugged him. 'Does it not seem incredible to you that you turn up in my life and end up in a woodturner's shed?'

'Not entirely. Pen loved the land around him; the earth, the trees. He was a natural woodturner. I came here to protect what he loved, and well, I really am doing that now, aren't I?' Clayton mused. 'I simply came into his life because we had something in common. Not that incredible. Hey, I've got one more surprise, but you have to come home for that one,' he teased.

'Clayton, what are you suggesting?'

She locked up the back door, and followed him home.

As she threw down her handbag on the kitchen table, something caught her attention. And there, in the lounge room, was a one-metre-high hand-made wooden rocking horse.

Bluey cried. 'It's beautiful!'

'Thought we might need one of these one day…' And with that, Clayton carried Bluey to the bedroom, kissing her all the way there.

An Open Book

Bluey was sitting at a round wooden table-for-two in the bookshop part of the café, sorting through her vast CD collection. The café had been closed for half an hour and she was enjoying the calm after the storm. It had been a frantically busy day, and this was the first time she'd been off her feet.

Tart apples mellowed in the oven, cinnamon sticks among them: their smells lingering in the air. In that very moment, life felt good.

Clayton sat back in his chair, a smile on his face, as he observed Bluey while she looked at each cover, turned it over and read the song titles, and then put it into one of her chosen piles: happy, sad, feel-good, love songs, melancholic, crooners, instrumentals.

From the day he met her, Clayton loved that Bluey was such an open book. It was impossible for her to have a thought or a feeling without it showing on her face. There was the way she wrinkled her nose when she wasn't sure about something, or furrowed her brow when trying to bite her tongue after hearing someone in the café say something she didn't agree with. And the way her dimples came alive and stretched half way up her cheeks when she was happy, or the manner in which she tossed her blonde hair over her shoulders when she was feeling a bit insecure.

He fell in love with every single one of her imperfections and her fragility, but Clayton Lansen wasn't fooled. Beneath it all, she was one tough cookie.

He adored her complexity, and how that innocent face covered a world of deep thoughts, kind intentions, wistful longings and shattered dreams.

A black Mercedes pulled up alongside the café, and two men in business suits stepped out. They stood looking across the bay for a few minutes, talking seriously, then walked up the café steps onto the verandah.

'What the hell are they doing here?' Bluey muttered under her breath.

Clayton looked up and was dismayed to see Melvin Jackson and Hugo Briggs.

'I thought this whole saga was over,' Clayton growled, opening the front door. 'Gentlemen, the café is closed now.' Clayton's words were firm. He caught Bluey out of the corner of his eye: hands on her hips, frowning. She looked like a bull marking his territory, ready to dig hooves into the ground and charge. Clayton walked over to her, and took her hand, ready to intervene if needed. He knew that Bluey would pummel them to the ground if she had to fight her corner.

'We believe you're the new owner of Pen Grille's land, Miss Miller. We'd like to negotiate with you to buy it,' Melvin Jackson drawled, taking a seat. But he'd no sooner sat down in his pressed business suit, briefcase on the table, than Bluey was next to him, hands on the back of the chair. 'The café's shut,' she said, indicating the door.

Hugo Briggs cleared his throat, and spoke up, his American South-West twang irritating her from the start. 'We'll offer you three times the market value,' he said. He was desperate to convince her.

'And we want to buy this café too, real sweet it is, plus the land by Bendigo Creek. We'll buy it all as one package.'

'No!' she yelled, shaking her head furiously, imagining the bodies of her beloved mother and Pen being covered by some high-rise building. 'I said we're closed, so please leave. And for the record, you're never welcome in this café again. Please go, or I'll call the police.'

It just so happened that Olivia was married to Hexham Brown, the local cop. They'd been high-school sweethearts, and Bluey knew that with just one phone call he'd be at the café quicker than you could say "corporate organisations taking over the world". Hexham was the big brother she never had.

Clayton had never seen her so furious. Despite the seriousness of the situation, he couldn't help but thinking: *that's my girl. You show 'em who's boss!*

'You have five seconds to get off my property.' Her hands were firmly on her hips. She was quite a sight. A force of Nature, more ferocious than a cyclone; not to be fooled with. But her pink, floral, ankle-length skirt, and her bare feet with silver anklets around the left ankle, indicated that she perhaps had a softer side than the one she was showing to the men in suits.

'Miss Miller, *three times* the market value! You'll never get an offer like that again,' Briggs insisted, as Jackson shook his head, defeated, walking out the door. 'We'll put the offer in writing. *Three times the market value!*'

'That land is now in a trust,' she called after them. 'It can never be sold off again.' She hoped it would be the last time she'd see them, but she could feel her heart racing like a train speeding through a tunnel. She wasn't sure if there was light at the end, or if she was driving into the dark. In a panic, she felt herself go dizzy, and grabbed the nearest chair.

'Are you okay, honey?' Clayton asked, kneeling beside her, and putting his arms around her shoulders.

'I hope that paperwork for the trust comes through from Hart soon,' she said, holding her hands out flat in front of her to indicate that she was shaking like a leaf. 'I hate that I just told a lie,' and she bit her bottom lip, and burrowed her eyebrows.

So that's what she looks like when she lies, he smiled to himself. But Clayton Lansen also knew it was a look he was unlikely to see very often. He filed it into his mental library of Bluey Facts, right up there with her favourite colour: purple; and favourite scent: freesia; and how her favourite song, *Fade Into You*, always left her in tears.

There were so many things he knew about her, like how she was ticklish behind her left knee, and loved to swim naked in Bendigo Creek, and her obsession with marinated artichokes. But there were also many things he didn't yet know about her. He had time. Plenty of time.

He carried in the dirty plates and cups to the kitchen and washed them up; and tidied a few bits and pieces while he was there.

When Clayton returned to the dining area, he stood at the doorway, smiling, and watched Bluey singing to a Dixie Chicks song as she continued sorting through her CD collection.

I wanna walk and not run,
I wanna skip and not fall
I wanna look at the horizon,
and not see a building standing tall
I wanna be the only one, for miles and miles
Except for maybe you, and your simple smile.

Was that the same woman who just tore strips off two middle-aged men? Yes, indeed. *His* woman.

The Fallow Field

Clayton gathered eight eager schoolkids around him, and held a clump of earth in his hands, letting it crumble softly between his fingers. They were on the top field of the land behind Maria Herring's house, and their goal was to turn it into a profitable market garden so they could earn pocket money.

'This field has been left fallow for a few years. It's important to do that on your land from time to time,' Clayton said. 'It gives it breathing space.'

That afternoon, the teenagers learnt about more than just soil and its properties. They found out that breaking up fallow ground, according to the life and times of Clayton Lansen, was like breaking your heart open, and allowing yourself to grow new seeds.

He talked about the times in his life when his heart had been so broken that he could hardly move on. The kids were sure they saw a tear in the corner of his eye. Clayton told them that you can only move on when you plant new seeds. 'You simply can't grow anything in a heart that's dry and hard. It needs to be softened; to be opened up like you do with fallow ground.'

Clayton talked about the process of clearing a field, and how our forefathers logged trees and rooted out stumps. 'After all the stumps are rooted up, they're piled together and burnt.'

Before he knew it, Clayton found himself talking in allegory again: *if you've got jealousy or hatred or bitterness in your heart, then you need to root it out before you can plant a new crop. New life won't grow in the shade of old stumps and trees.*

The teenagers learnt about ploughing, not just of the soil in the field, but directing it towards the hard places in their hearts.

It certainly hadn't been Clayton's intention to become a spiritual mentor to these kids, but he found the words flowed easily. They'd come into his life for a reason, and he into their lives.

Each day that the teenagers laboured on the land, they learnt more. Clayton could feel their excitement building. This wasn't just a job, but was fast becoming a way of life: a welcome break from the routine of school and insurmountable piles of homework. They learnt that rocks need to be removed, and sometimes it feels impossible to shift them. They learnt techniques such as leverage, digging and horse power.

'When you've tried everything you can to shift a rock and it won't budge, that's when you need to find someone to help you...someone who isn't judgemental, and can act as a mentor.'

Soil or soul? Clayton found they were interchangeable, and he discovered far more about himself than he ever expected to up in that old field.

As the weeks turned to months, the students saw signs of their hard work come to fruition. Baskets of vegetables sold on the steps of Bluey's Café, and the kids felt empowered.

Clayton helped them set up a cooperative, with each of them working for the same pay, and sharing equally in decision making. They invested some of the profits back into purchasing seeds, tools, seaweed fertiliser, and bags and baskets for selling produce.

Bluey offered them recipes to feature their vegetable of the week, and some of the students wrote them up and placed copies with the weekly newsletter they put into the paper bags containing vegetables.

Reg the Veg was even supportive of his young rivals, and offered to buy surplus produce from them to sell to the restaurants he supplied.

The Sun was high in the noonday sky one Saturday as the teens and Clayton sought the shade of some eucalyptus trees at the edge of the field so they could quietly eat lunch.

'How do you think the plants feel when it's this hot?' he asked. None of them answered. They weren't sure if it was another one of Clayton's trick questions, or a gentle sermon. He glided between both with ease.

'When you're kneeling around a vegetable pulling weeds or checking it for bugs or watering it, try and be the plant. Put yourself in their roots. Which birds and animals are around? Which insects? Pay attention, when you can, and notice how much is going on around you. Close your eyes if you need to. You might hear the crows in the trees making a racket, but if you listen real carefully, you might even hear the stem of the plant moving in the breeze.'

He finished the beetroot and rocket rye sandwich that Bluey had made for their lunches, and said 'In this field, we learn about patience, and letting go of expectations. None of us knows how these vegetables will turn out. One storm could ruin the lot! Too much rain coming down off Briar Ridge could wash them all away. No rain for months could kill them off. No matter how much we water them, nothing is as good for them as rain falling steadily for a few days, seeping deep down into the soil.'

He got up, wiped his beetroot-stained fingers onto the front of his bleach-faded denim jeans, and said 'Today we're going to learn about growth and renewal. Here's a bucket of compost from Bluey's Café. We're going to build a few compost heaps from these old pallets I brought up. In the compost, we'll put leaves, kitchen waste, grass clippings, weeds…essentially anything that will rot down.'

Katie Jennings, a shy fifteen-year-old girl who'd developed quite a crush on Clayton, spoke up in barely a whisper. 'Can we bring compost here from our home?'

'That'd be brilliant,' Clayton smiled.

She'd hardly said a word since working here, but he could tell she was passionate about every aspect of the project. He was oblivious to her passion for him, though.

'Coffee grinds, egg shells, paper, fruit and vegetable peelings. They all work well,' he said.

Four of the boys helped Clayton to lift the pallets up, and they nailed them together to form large, open-topped boxes.

'Composting means nothing gets wasted, not a single apple or onion skin. What happens when they all end up there is nothing short of a miracle. It's what we call a transformation. What we're doing is taking yesterday and making tomorrow!' he grinned. 'When I look back on my life, I see that there was a lot of stuff to be composted. Old memories, mistakes, bad habits, even old habits. We can sit back and regret all these things, or we can do something about it.'

'Compost it?' Katie asked.

'Yeah. That's right. It's as simple as asking yourself: *what can I learn from all this?*'

'So it becomes part of a new cycle?' Katie asked hesitantly.

'Yeah, so it can lead to new growth.'

Clayton thought he heard her whisper, 'Wow'.

'And of course, you can *literally* compost it. Shall we try it?' Clayton went to the jeep and pulled out a pad of paper.

He passed a piece to each person. 'When I've finished with my pen, I'll give it to someone else, and we can all take turns.' Clayton scribbled down some words and said out loud: 'Today, I compost my bad habit of always eating three helpings of whatever Bluey cooks.' And then he threw the paper into the newly erected compost bin. The kids laughed, but they got the message.

'You might think it can take a while to let go of bad habits, but don't give up. If it feels like nothing's changed, simply tell yourself: *I've composted that!*'

The kids took to composting likes ducks to water, and Clayton smiled to himself whenever they turned up to work and stood by the compost bins throwing in bits of paper.

He'd been devoted to his varied life path of woodturning, forest ranging, mediating between land owners and big business, but he found that as each day passed, working with these teenagers was the most rewarding work he'd ever done. He was nurturing them while they nurtured the vegetables.

Special Delivery

Logie Thim's appaloosa gelding was tied to a post of the café verandah. Logie drank his morning coffee while chatting across the table to Mrs Hetherington and old Miss Ryers. He stopped by every morning on his way to the far end of the bay.

Ford Marks and his wife, Narelle, were eating peach cupcakes with their spiced chai lattes.

Suzanne and Felicity came by for mango smoothies after teaching their morning aerobics class at the leisure centre, and Mellie Bridge was sitting in the bookshop reading *Why Good Women Love Bad Men*, and sniffing into her tissue. She had two other books picked out that she intended to buy: *Men are from Mars, Women are from Venus* and *Women Who Love Too Much*.

To Bluey, it was just a regular morning at the café: familiar faces, the usual conversations overheard: weather, cost of living, love affairs. Yep, the same old, same old. That is, until she saw Ivan Bourke get off his postal-delivery bike, looking uneasy.

He was a tall man, but today he didn't seem his full height.

'What's wrong, Ivan?' she asked nervously, as he stooped towards her at the counter.

'Mail like this never brings good news,' he said, passing over an envelope that she needed to sign for.

Atient and Oxion Solicitors, she read the embossed gold print in the top corner of the envelope. It was a large Sydney-based firm.

'Why is this bad news? I don't even know these solicitors,' she said, shrugging her shoulders. 'Hart's my solicitor. Has been for ten years.'

Bluey signed Ivan's form, and watched him slink over to a nearby table for two.

She left Olivia in charge of the counter, and went and sat down with him. Ripping open the envelope, she began to read:

```
Dear Miss Miller,
Jackson-Briggs Incorporated has
commenced legal action to secure
the land formerly belonging
to the late Pen Grille, on the
grounds that he had a moment of
confusion when it came to signing
his signature. Charges include
unlawful possession of the land,
and trespassing.
```

Bluey sat in stunned silence. The nightmare was continuing. She passed the letter to Ivan, and by the time he'd read those few words, he too looked like a ghost.

'We won't let them take that property from you, Bluey. Every single person in this bay will back you up. We'll form a human shield if we have to,' he promised.

'It's going to take more than that,' she said, standing tall and breathing deeply. 'No more Miss Goody-Two-Shoes Miller! *This is war*! Olivia, hold the fort,' she called out over her shoulder, and jogged down the bay towards Hart Joiner and Sons, Solicitors.

'I don't have an appointment,' she said half apologetically to the receptionist, 'but this is urgent.'

'Just one moment,' said the shy girl behind her oversized glasses. She scampered over to Hart's door, knocking sharply three times, and entered when she heard him say yes.

'Miss Miller to see you. She says it's urgent.'

'Send her in.'

'Hart, I'm so sorry for barging in, but this couldn't wait,' she said, holding out the offensive message.

Reading it over, he looked up and smiled.

'It's just bluff, Bluey.'

'How can you be so sure?' she asked.

'It would cost them a fortune to take you to court.'

'They've got the money! They were offering me three times the market value of the land.'

'Really? Why didn't you tell me?'

'Clayton and I sent them packing. I told them it was in trust, and couldn't be sold.'

'Oh.' He sighed, and then looked up from the letter into her eyes, back at the letter, and up at her again. 'It could take months for the land to legally be set up as a trust. It's a slow process. I can't hurry that up. In the meantime, we need to find a way to stall these guys.' His tone was grave.

'You're scaring me, Hart.'

'Right, what we need is any evidence that you can think of that might prove that Pen didn't want them to have the land. We've got his last will and testament, but they could argue that it was six months old at the time of his death. Legally, he would have had to update it once the land was in Jackson-Briggs hands, but obviously he didn't get a chance to do either.'

Hart sat for a few moments studying every word of the letter.

'I'll send a brief reply, and do what I can to stall them. Was there anything, anything at all, in Pen's personal possessions when you were clearing out his home that might indicate he had no intention of selling to them, or that his intentions were for you to have the land? Anything at all, Bluey? You have to think really hard.'

Bluey drew a blank. 'I'll have to think about it. Right now, my brain is on overload. This is not how I was expecting the day to go.'

Hart tapped the gold fountain pen on his mahogany desk with nervous agitation. 'Every person in the bay could be a witness to Pen's long-term love of the land, and his rejection of big business. That'd make the court case run on and on if each of them has to take the stand,' Hart smiled, feeling quite good at the cunning plan evolving in his head.

'Do we really want to involve the whole town in this?' Bluey asked.

'The whole town *is* involved. No one wants this bay filled with high-rise buildings. Not a single person. Of course they're involved. Name me one person who doesn't come by your café at least once a week.'

She couldn't think of anyone.

'Okay, so what now?' she asked nervously.

'Just see if you can think of anything to indicate Pen's intentions, and I'll draft a letter. And, one other thing, try not to think about it too much.'

She raised her eyebrows. How could she *not* think of the potential destruction of the bay?

As Bluey walked back to the café, another thought occurred to her: grandmother. She'd sold her home, and moved her entire life to live at Mountain View Lodge. Bluey felt anger seep through every blood vessel in her body. *No way in hell are they making Granny move!* she thought to herself.

For the next few months, letters were exchanged between Hart, and Atient and Oxion Solicitors.

'Hart's got your back, honey,' Clayton said kindly one Sunday morning as he saw Bluey chewing her fingernails nervously.

'The court case starts in one week. Of course I'm nervous! What proof do I have that Pen didn't want to do this? I know you're a witness, as is every other person in the bay, but I'm scared it won't be enough. I just can't believe this nightmare is still going on!'

'Honey, you once said to me that your heart told you that you'd be staying here. Between that heart, and the legal Hart, let's trust that everything will be okay.'

'God I wish you weren't so calm and casual about this. This is my life!' she said, tension filling the air of the kitchen.

Clayton gently placed his hands on her shoulders. 'This is *our* life. We're in this together, remember? I don't want them to take the land any more than you do. Don't you remember the reason I came to Calico Bay in the first place? If I appear calm, it's only so I can keep my wits about me. Living off nervous energy isn't going to help anyone. Now, let me make you a chamomile tea, and then today we're going to go up to the mountains and just forget about everything.' He wiped a lone tear from her cheek.

She nodded her head in agreement.

Secret Love

Monday morning came around the corner just a little too quickly for Bluey. She needed more time. Another six days, and she'd be standing in a courtroom fighting for her life. Clayton's life. Granny's life. The life of the bay. It was all she could do to keep breathing. Jackson-Briggs Incorporated had big money and big lawyers. They'd excavate every legal loophole, burning money like there was no tomorrow. And what did she have? Hart was offering his services for free!

The atmosphere in the dining area was tense all week long. Everyone for miles around knew what was happening, and each one had gone to Hart's office to write a witness statement. But it wouldn't be enough, Bluey knew that. It was just wishful thinking.

By Friday afternoon, she'd had enough. The café would be shut all next week during the trial. Perhaps she should just give in now and save any more stress. She could sell the café and start again somewhere, even in another town.

After the last well-wishing customers left, Bluey sat down and cried. There was so much pent-up stress and anger, that it finally reached tipping point. Something had to give.

When she'd recovered, Bluey poured herself some fresh home-made lemonade and looked for a CD to play. She needed to wind down before heading home and dumping her stress on Clayton.

'No, not you,' she said to at least thirty CDs before arriving at Doris Day.

She recalled how much her mother loved to sing along to one particular song while doing the ironing on a Sunday morning. She'd iron; Pen would mow.

Once I had a secret love
That lived within the heart of me
All too soon my secret love
Became impatient to be free

Bluey smiled to herself, and wondered: was Mum trying to make me guess? Did she hint what was going on? How could I have been so blind?

So many questions, racing around her mind! It was as if her mother were here, right now, in the café, trying to talk to her once again.

So I told a friendly star
The way that dreamers often do
Just how wonderful you are
And why I'm so in love with you

Why didn't you just tell me, Mum? Why did you have to keep it a secret? Bluey wondered.

Now I shout it from the highest hills
Even told the golden daffodils

'You really wanted everyone to know, didn't you?' Bluey said, recalling the diary entry where her mother had written that she'd be proud to walk down the bay as Mrs Grille.

At last my heart's an open door
And my secret love's no secret any more

'Well, you're wrong there! It's still a bloody secret!' Bluey said, turning the CD player off, grabbing her backpack, and riding her scooter home.

'Thought we might eat on the beach tonight,' Clayton said, smiling brightly as she came in the back door.

'Sounds wonderful!' she said, artificially lighting up her face so he wouldn't sense her sadness, but Clayton knew her too well.

'Honey, we're not in court today. Today is a day that is calling out for us to go and eat on the beach. Let's just do that, and not give all our power away to those men in suits.'

She smiled, this time a bit more sincerely. 'Have I got time for a shower first?'

'Sure you have. I'll pack these picnic things into the jeep. Don't hurry,' he said, whistling on his way outside.

A few hours passed, and they ate tomato and basil tart, cucumber and lime salad, and sipped crisp Chardonnay. They lay on the sand, holding each other's hands, and watching the sky turn from day to night.

'I remember Pen telling me the legend of the night sky. I learnt so much from him. He always had time for me. Time to tell me stories. Time to share myths and legends of the bush. He said that the Milky Way was known as the river, and Alakitja was a large codfish. He was a clever fish, and managed to avoid the fish traps of the sky people. As he swam, Alakitja made his way past an untold number of white water lilies. The lilies shone so brightly so that those of us on Earth would see them. We call them stars. When Alakitja finished his journey, he hid from the Sun. Two brothers created mountains and rivers on Earth, and this was hungry work, so they looked high and low for food. One look at Alakitja and they started throwing spears at him! They killed him, and shared the fish between them, but each cooked it over their own campfire.' Bluey pointed at the sky, and said, 'See, you can still see their campfires to this day. One is Delta Crucis and the other is Gamma Crucis. And those two bright stars of the cross are Alpha and Beta Centauri.

They're the brothers.'

'And what about Alakitja? Where is he?' Clayton asked.

'In that dark area.'

In the silence, they watched the stars twinkling, and the sudden rush of a falling star caught their breath. 'Make a wish!' Clayton whispered.

'I have,' Bluey replied.

She gently hummed *Secret Love*.

'I'm so glad our love isn't a secret,' Clayton murmured, as he pulled her closer for a slow, long kiss.

'So am I,' she replied. 'So am I.'

As they packed up their food containers and blanket, Bluey asked, 'Do you think Mum's diary would be any good as evidence? It's just that it was written before Pen died and reflected on their conversations and how he vowed never to sell the land to Jackson-Briggs. *Over my dead body* were his exact words.'

'Why didn't we think of this before?' he asked, scooping her into his arms.

'I did. I have! But it feels wrong to share it. Her diary is private!' Bluey said, scared to share her mother's deepest feelings with the world.

Judgement Day

The judge determined the mood in the courtroom, and called the money-hungry team of lawyers to heel. There were no less than eight barristers and lawyers for Jackson-Briggs Incorporated.

Hart sat like an injured lone bird on the beach, trying to hold back the tide about to wash over Calico Bay like a tsunami. He hadn't counted on such underhand tactics.

A reporter from the Calico Bay Chronicle was scribbling in his notepad, and journalists from the city were typing into their iPads.

Calico Bay didn't have a courthouse of its own. They were in Rallervale, and ironically, it was opposite the Oak Lane Orphanage.

The courthouse was packed, and the judge listened to arguments from both sides. Jackson-Briggs argued that Pen had signed the papers, but in a moment of confusion was thinking of an old friend and wrote her name.

Hart argued that he was grief stricken for the love of his life, who'd only recently died. There were gasps and whispers from the crowd: *Lovers? Pen and Emily? No!*

The judge demanded silence from the gallery, but still the whispers continued.

On Thursday, Bluey was called to the stand. She hoisted the heavy tome of Emily's diary along with her.

'I'd like to read from my late mother's diary. I believe every one of Pen's intentions is clear here.'

'Inadmissible!' came the cries from the Jackson-Briggs team. 'This wasn't submitted as evidence!'

'Let her speak,' the judge said sternly.

Bluey stumbled over her first few words, shaking as she was from the terror of standing before the firing squad in their navy-blue suits and ridiculous wigs. She found Clayton's eyes in the sea of faces, and anchored herself in his love. *You can do this*. She heard his voice in her head, and like a warrior goddess fought for her land with everything she had.

'A diary is personal, so personal, in fact, that it shouldn't be read by anyone but the person who writes in it. For some reason, my mother expressly wanted me to have her diary after she died.' She looked at the judge so he could see her sincerity. He put down his pen and paid attention. 'I've read things in this diary about myself, about the people of Calico Bay, and about my mother, that I simply didn't know before. It's been such a revelation...'

'Your honour, what's this got to do with us acquiring that property? She's wasting court time!'

'Silence. This is my courtroom! I'll decide just who is wasting my time!' And with a swift thump on the table with his fist, he made it quite clear who was in charge. 'Continue, Miss Miller.'

'My mother and Pen Grille were in love with each other since primary school. Many people in this room will be surprised by this, but probably no more surprised than me. After all, I shared the same roof as my mother, and had no idea!'

'Your honour?' pleaded another lawyer in frustration.

The judge didn't say a word. His eyes said: *shut up!*

'I believe Pen died of a heart attack as a consequence of the harassment he received from being bombarded daily by Jackson-Briggs!'

Yells and cries from the packed courtroom brought chaos. The judge hit the table. 'Silence! Miss Miller, what proof do you have of this?' The judge looked at Hart. 'Why hasn't Miss Miller been advised to counter-sue?'

Hart looked lost for words, and flailed around his notes. He had no idea that Bluey believed such a thing.

'My mother wrote about Pen's high blood pressure, and how Doctor Baker was really concerned. He'd always had perfectly normal blood pressure, but in the months before his heart attack, according to my mother's diary, he received daily phone calls and visits at all hours of the day pressuring him to sell.' Bluey said, suddenly aware that her nerves had given way to something else. She had found her voice. Emily Miller was right beside her, urging her on.

'Do you know, by any chance, who his doctor was? I would like to see medical records,' the judge said, writing down some notes.

Doctor Baker stood up in the back of the crowded courtroom. 'I was Pen Grille's doctor, your honour. I can vouch for what Miss Miller is saying to the court. I can provide records for you.'

The judge nodded to the doctor, and then indicated for Bluey to continue.

There were several entries relating to Jackson-Briggs, including one where he vowed never to sell. His words were: "over my dead body". Silence slipped through the court room.

'I was hoping to have this case wrapped up by tomorrow afternoon, but given this new information, I feel I have no choice but to suspend it until I've had time to read this diary, or to throw it out of court right now.'

The legal team for Jackson-Briggs was agitated, and the men clambered over each other's files like furious ants escaping a damaged anthill.

The judge called for Hart and the head barrister of the Jackson-Briggs legal team to adjourn in his private chamber.

'This is ridiculous. That girl could sue you for causing Pen Grille's death, and if Hart was any sort of lawyer,' the judge said, staring him right in the eye, 'there are probably half a dozen other charges that could be thrown your way. It's not my place to say what they are, but you've got five minutes to decide if this case is worth continuing. Five minutes, and if this does continue, you better make sure you win.'

The judge ordered them out of the room, and sat with

his head in his hands. It was obvious to him that Pen was a grieving man, and had no intention of selling his land. The diary was more than enough evidence of that, but was it enough for him to throw the case out of court? He wanted to honour Bluey and Emily Miller's privacy and not force her to read passages out from it, but he also knew it was cutting legal corners to have Bluey's say-so in a courtroom. He prayed that Jackson-Briggs would just pull out.

'We're too close to give in now,' Briggs bellowed to his legal team out in the corridor. 'We're not giving in because of some diary! Why should a dead woman be considered the definitive witness? I'm not paying you lot the big bucks for nothing. Now go and do your job!'

The judge sighed. This was not the outcome he'd urged.

'I would like both sides to take some time and we'll reconvene on Monday morning.' The judge walked out of the room, shaking his head from side to side.

Bluey slumped in the chair. 'I can't believe this. How can this possibly be running into a second week? Everyone in the bay has spoken up as a witness. What else can we do?' she asked Hart, as everyone dispersed from the room. She looked around. What a sombre environment: brown walls, brown furniture, cheap brown carpet. She thought of the colourful world of her life, from the red bottlebrush and yellow wattle flowers to the buttery hues of the Huon-pine furniture that Clayton had carved, and the vibrant vegetables nestled in the willow baskets of the café, and the red sunsets of the bay, and the black-velvet night skies. How could any of those lawyers and businessmen sit in such a dark and miserable room and understand what Bluey was fighting for? She felt like a one-woman force against mass corporate destruction. Hart must have picked her thoughts.

'We're all on your side, Bluey. You're not in this alone,' he said, gently touching her hand.

'He's right, honey. This is everyone's fight, not just yours,' Clayton added.

'The judge will want you to read from the diary. He also thinks we should counter-sue. It's a possibility, but then the onus is on you to initiate a costly court case. Personally, I wouldn't recommend it. At least... not at this point. Let's see what we can do with what we've got. How would you feel about me reading the diary over the weekend so I can see if there are any points specific to getting this case dropped?'

Bluey's life flashed before her eyes. She liked Hart. She liked him a lot. He was a good man. But she knew if she passed over her mother's diary, that she wouldn't be able to censor the parts of her life that she'd rather forget.

'What's wrong, honey' Clayton asked, concern making his heart beat rapidly. What didn't she want Hart to see?

'Okay.' She sighed deeply. 'Do NOT let it out of your sight, and do not let anyone else read it.'

'Sure,' he said. And then, more seriously: 'I promise.'

Reluctantly she handed over the weighty volume. Her heart sank into the ugliest carpet she'd ever stood on. Bluey's land, her café, Bendigo Creek and Maria Herring's new home all rested in Hart's hands.

'You guys have a good weekend. Don't think about this. You've done everything you can; the rest is up to me. Please, try not to give it another thought,' Hart said, packing up his briefcase and armful of folders.

They waved him off, and Clayton said 'He's right, you know. We've done everything we can. Promise me we'll have fun this weekend?' he pleaded gently. 'How about I take you up to Rainbow Falls for a walk and a picnic?'

'Sounds lovely,' she smiled, determined to let go of the load on her shoulders.

Kind Hands

Sunday morning skipped along with the sea breeze, and as bright and bubbly as Bluey Miller herself on a good day. Today was a good day. She sat on the tyre swing beneath the old pepperina tree, admiring the view. Pen had hung up the swing when she was seven years old. Clayton turned off the lawnmower when he saw her, and asked 'What are you grinning about?'

The aroma of fresh-cut grass was one of Bluey's favourite smells. It was the scent of security, and a loving childhood. As the church bells rang out over Calico Bay, she said 'Every Sunday morning, Pen would be here to cut the grass. Him and the church bells, *every* Sunday morning. You could set your watch to it!' She laughed a little. 'Watching you just brought it all back.'

She looked at Clayton's hands, and thought of Pen again. 'You've got similar hands, too,' she marvelled, 'They're kind hands.'

'Bluey Miller, what on Earth are *kind* hands?'

And there was that smile that made him fall in love on the verandah of Bluey's Café all those months ago. Her rosebud lips stretched across her tanned face; blonde hair sitting around her shoulders, and wispy fringes endearingly settling just over her eyebrows. But then, her smile faded as quickly as a dog down a rabbit hole.

'They're hands that will never hurt me.' She hesitated for a moment. 'Hands I can trust,' Bluey said it in such a serious way that he started to feel concerned.

'Honey, of course I'd never hurt you. Why would you even think that?' he asked. Sweat dripped down his unshaven cheeks, a symptom of labouring with the lawnmower in the morning heat.

'I know you wouldn't. I know,' she whispered. 'I've just never thought about your hands in that way before. You and Pen. You have so much in common, and as each day passes I see that more and more.'

'I talk more than him, though, don't I?' Clayton laughed, touching her cheek with his grass-stained thumb: softly, so softly. 'I would never, ever hurt you,' he said slowly, hoping she'd absorb his promise, and realising there was a lot to Bluey that he had yet to learn. But Clayton Lansen was a patient man. He'd spent years mediating, learning to listen to people, letting them have the time and space to speak. Years of learning to read between the lines. He was starting to get a sense of her story. His heart felt leaden at the thought that Bluey had known unkind hands. It flattened him to think someone could do anything harmful to her. It was like a grown man using a steel-capped boot to crush a beautiful butterfly, and squishing it into the concrete, just for the fun of it: just because they could. Pointless.

To Clayton, everything about Bluey Miller was beautiful: she was trusting, kind, loving, open, vivacious and friendly. Clayton had never met anyone with such enthusiasm and joy for life, and he reminded himself that he entered her life during the dark night of her soul: the loss of a parent. But he'd watched her unfurl, like a fern in Spring, during the past few months, wearing grief like a heavy leather harness, but still trying to gallop with all the glee of a new lamb, as was her nature. He knew it had been tough for her, and had held her through many middle-of-the-night cries. Clayton admired her spirit. *But unkind hands?* That made him feel ill to the core.

He put the lawnmower in the tin shed, had a shower, and said 'Come back to bed, honey. It's Sunday morning. There's nowhere else we need to be.'

Rainy Days and Mondays

Rain spat with contempt at Bluey's bedroom window, and Monday battered itself head first into the strong winds.

'Don't let the weather get you down,' Clayton said when she entered the kitchen.

He had prepared grilled tomatoes and field mushrooms for their breakfast.

Towel-drying her hair, Bluey said 'Not the best of omens, though, is it?'

'Depends how you see it,' he smiled. 'It could be that it means the rain will wash away the negativity that Jackson-Briggs has brought here, and the wind will scoot them out of town quicker than you can say *tree hugger and proud of it!*'

He placed the plates of food onto the wooden kitchen table.

'Nothing wrong with tree huggers,' she muttered when she took a mouthful of mushrooms.

'Exactly. Now, eat the rest of your breakfast up. You'll need all your energy for the day ahead.'

Bluey decided against wearing a suit to the courthouse. She had worn them all last week, and didn't like it one bit. She'd spent five days of her life trying to fit into the world of law-making, business suits, court-talk etiquette, and she'd finally had enough. Today she was going as Bluey Miller: café owner, daughter, granddaughter, friend, lover, and tree hugger.

She wore her favourite lime-green sundress, and let her hair down. Around her neck was a wooden pendant that Pen had carved for her sixteenth birthday.

'You look beautiful!' Clayton said, giving her a wolf whistle as she entered the lounge room.

'My mother sewed me this dress for Olivia's wedding,' she smiled. 'I've got great memories with this dress.'

With Pen, Emily and Clayton by her side, she was

ready: ready for a rainy day, a Monday, and a fight-for-your-life day.

Hart greeted them by the steps of the courtroom. One look in his eyes, and Bluey knew. She *knew* that Hart knew everything about her life, or at least, that is, her life through her mother's eyes: the good, the bad and the downright rotten. He greeted her with a big hug. Clayton sensed something. Hart had always been friendly, but slightly guarded by his professional code of conduct. Where was this hug coming from? Had he given up? Clayton was confused.

The judge began the day recapping arguments for both sides.

Bluey intuited that he was irritated to be back here, and wanted it all over as much as she did.

When she was called to the stand to read selected excerpts from the diary, she was sure she noticed a smile and a twinkle in the judge's eye when she playfully swished the skirt of her long dress.

Hart had marked out several sections of the diary with hot-pink Post-it notes to indicate what should be read. He was careful to avoid anything that would indicate private areas of Bluey's past. She began to read:

Pen has been under daily stress from some development company called Jackson-Briggs. They phone him every day and late into the night; they send letters, and they turn up uninvited on his doorstep. They want his land, all two-hundred acres of it. Pen thought it was a joke that they'd applied to the council for planning permission, several years before, and got it! It's not even their land, and yet they've got permission to build a massive development on there once it's acquired.

"Over my dead body," he grunted to me today. "They'll never get that property."

She paused, wiped a tear with Clayton's cotton handkerchief, then read another entry:

Pen was in a prickly mood all day. When he finally spoke he said "Jackson-Briggs banged on my door at midnight. Bloody midnight! Offered me twice the market price. I said 'which part of I'm never selling don't you understand', and slammed the door in their faces. This is harassment! I don't know how to get rid of them."

He was silent for a while. He could probably tell that I was too frail to be of much emotional comfort. And then he said, rather solemnly, "I updated my will today. I'm leaving everything to Bluey. When you're gone, she'll be the only family I have left in the whole world. If anything should happen to me, I want that land, that house, Briar Ridge, Bendigo Creek ~ the whole lot ~ to be in the hands of a woman who loves it as much as I do. I know Bluey will look after it. And I know my grandmother would have approved."

Bluey looked up, tears prickling her eyes, a lump catching in her already-raspy throat. There wasn't a resident of Calico Bay sitting in the seats before her who wasn't wiping their eyes, or sniffing into a tissue, or hugging their partner.

'That's enough, Miss Miller. You may return to your seat,' the judge said. 'I'm going to retire to my chamber, and we'll reconvene at 11am.' He swiftly left the room, and hushed talking permeated the dull and lifeless courtroom air.

Bluey felt as if she'd been admonished. She'd barely read any of the many excerpts which Hart had picked out. Dejected, she sat down beside Hart and looked at him hopelessly. Clayton put his arms around her.

'Look, let's go out and get some fresh air,' Clayton said. 'Come on.' He led her by the hand, and they walked down the steps of the courthouse into the misty rain.

Tears trickled down her face. This was it. The fight was over. The only choice left was to sell the café or watch a sea of high rises be built around her. Over the road, Oak Lane Orphanage lured her. She walked across the shaded street, Clayton in hot pursuit. By the time he caught up, she was sobbing. Before her were two large wrought-iron gates. The words of her mother's diary rang through her head.

She stood at the black wrought-iron gates with her little chubby, dimpled fingers wrapped firmly around two poles. In one hand, was a little blue blanket that she hung onto for dear life. Blonde hair tousled around her shoulders, and she looked up at me and asked 'Will you be my Mummy?'

Bluey couldn't stop crying. Defining life moments happening on the same street: she was at the mercy of the hands of fate.

'This is unfair!' she sobbed. 'So unfair!'

Clayton held her securely. 'Whatever happens now, you need to stop fighting. You've done everything you can. Pen would have been so proud of you, and by god so would your mother. *I'm* so proud of you. All you can do is surrender to the situation, and trust that whatever happens, whether that means being amid their development or selling up, it's all for the best. I know those choices don't feel like it, but you have to go with the flow now.'

He felt washed out. He wanted to give Bluey the whole world, and yet his hands were tied. The Bluey he had grown to love—feisty, happy, gregarious, thoughtful—had all but disappeared this past week. She'd been replaced by an ashen ghost.

'You got through your mum's illness, and her death. And Pen's death. Bluey Miller, you can get through the rest of this day.'

He tried to buoy her up, but she had a concrete weight dragging her mind down.

They stood by the orphanage for some time, watching the children at play. 'Do you think it's cruel to bring children into this world?' she asked.

'Cruel?'

'Yes. We don't know what life has in store for anyone, do we?'

'Your parents brought you into this world because they loved you. And look at how much love you've given in your life. Where's the cruelty in that?' he asked. He knew she was in a dark place, and the only way out of it was if she changed her mind about the situation.

'We best go back, honey. The judge will return in ten minutes.'

'You know, I think I'm just going to go back to the bay. I know what his answer will be. I don't want to be there and give that Jackson lot the pleasure of seeing me break down,' she said. 'Can you and Granny get a lift back to Calico Bay with Hart?'

'Honey? Don't give up yet,' he pleaded, but it was no use. She had given up. Clayton gave Bluey the keys to the jeep, and kissed her on the forehead. 'Drive slowly,' he pleaded.

The Scales of Justice

Bluey parked the jeep on the roadside, and walked around the back of the café. The rain had perked up the vegetables and salad leaves. She felt a spark of gratitude. Despite her complete neglect of the café over the past week, somehow the plants got looked after. The grey clouds pushed each other across the sky, making way for some afternoon sunshine. She sat on the back doorstep, admiring the thriving vegetable gardens, and looked over to the trees lining Bendigo Creek. 'I'm sorry, Mum, and I'm sorry, Pen,' she said. 'I'm so sorry. I really tried.'

Bluey wiped her eyes and went into the kitchen. Olivia had left it spic-and-span clean, with a handwritten list of suggestions for the menu.

They hadn't done a vegetable order for a week, so she'd only be able to use the ones growing out the back, unless she headed up to the top field. But she was sidetracked by the weighing scales on the bench. So many thoughts came to her: right, wrong, balance, fairness. They were all associated with the scales of justice. She thought of the zodiac sign, Libra, the only sign ruled by an inanimate object: the scales. Keith Kunner came into her mind, and she grabbed her belly as a wave of nausea brought sickness to the centre of her being. Sure, justice had been done, if that's what you could call it. But it would never take away her painful memories. Justice didn't make her feel like a winner. Not once did she feel victorious. Bluey recalled the week-long court case where he was held accountable for his despicable actions. Every second of her ordeal with him during that nasty episode was made open for public consumption. She found strength alongside the many other women who chose to follow her lead and speak up during the trial. Testifying against his violence, the judge was left in no doubt that Keith Kunner needed to be behind bars for many years. There were a lot of times after the court case when Bluey felt that people treated her differently. To Calico Bay, she was the voice which said: treat women with respect, or watch out! The phone ringing made her jump out of her skin, and back to the present moment: vegetables! She let the phone ring off the hook.

Bluey decided that perhaps she'd take a drive up to the top field after all. Her grandmother was still at the courthouse, so there was no risk of anyone stopping her for conversation.

The top field was thriving, and Bluey found herself smiling at just how much the teenage cooperative had achieved in recent months. No wonder Clayton had felt such joy working with them. Loneliness haunted her heart as she thought of having to move these young people on. Each one of them had turned up to the court house—skipping six days of school with special permission—so they could lend their support. Bluey felt she was letting down so many people: the teenagers, grandmother, Pen, Emily, Clayton, Hart: everyone, including herself.

Into her trug she gathered an assortment of fresh vegetables. She was walking by the compost heap, and noticed bits of paper on top with writing on them. 'That's odd,' she thought, and couldn't help but pick one up. She recognised the writing straight away, even though it was partially smudged by the recent rain. It was Clayton's handwriting.

'Today I compost Jackson-Briggs and leave them in the past.'

'Compost? Compost Jackson-Briggs?' she laughed out loud. 'He's so very sweet.'

She picked up another piece of paper, but didn't recognise the writing. 'Today I compost any thoughts of this land being sold off.'

Bluey couldn't believe what she was reading. She read through the other seven pieces of paper. They each said something similar. *Compost bad men. Compost big business. Compost greed. Compost Bluey's sadness so Clayton can be happy again.* She almost choked on her tears. They really were all on her side. She wasn't alone. This fight hadn't been about her. Clayton was right. She had to surrender now. She had to choose whether to sell or make the best of things. But what about her grandmother? Sure, Maria Herring could come and live with them. The house was big enough. But...

Bluey could barely see through her tears by the time she pulled up at the café. All these cars! *We're not even open*, she muttered, at the thought of so many tourists intruding on her privacy. And then she noticed a few familiar cars amongst them, including Hart's BMW. She walked around to the front of the café. The verandah was full of people, spilling out down the steps and onto the road. From an ocean of faces, she caught Clayton's eyes.

'What's going on?' she asked, still so fragile and tender from her trip by Clayton's compost heap.

'Come and sit down, honey,' he said, and people made way so she could walk up the stairs. Olivia had opened the café, and every seat was taken.

'What's going on, Clayton?'

'Sit,' he said, pulling up a chair for her. 'The judge said he carefully weighed up both sides of the argument, and said that he found no compelling reasons to believe that Pen wanted to sell his property to Jackson-Briggs.' He could see that she wasn't comprehending the news. 'He's ordered an injunction which prevents Jackson-Briggs ever making contact with you again in any form.'

Clayton put his hands on her shoulders. 'Bluey, have you heard what I said? We won!'

Bluey was dazed. She looked around the room. The sea of faces started to make sense. The teenagers were there, sipping milkshakes, and Maria Herring was drinking tea. Ivan Bourke was eating a baguette, and Mrs

Hetherington was sipping hot chocolate. Bluey's whole life was before her, and any minute she'd wake up from the dream. Any minute, Clayton would say "it's time to sell". But she didn't wake up. Applause began closest to her, and spread out onto the verandah and onto the roadside.

'Three cheers for Bluey!' yelled Hart, uncharacteristically extroverted.

Bluey looked at Clayton again in disbelief. 'We've won?'

'Oh yes honey, we've won.' He held her for quite some time, not wanting to let her go. But he had to, because Clayton wasn't the only one who wanted to wrap his arms around her in happiness. The celebrations continued right into the night, with dancing, singing and more coffee sold than she'd normally sell in a week.

Mother to Daughter

Dear diary...
So, this is goodbye. I trust that one day Bluey
will read this diary, and come to know me
better. To see who I was as a woman and a lover,
not just as a mother.

We're so much more than just mothers, and yet
motherhood is everything. At least, it was for
me.

I pray that she finds a love as whole and true as
the one I found with Pen. I hope she finds a man
who is kind and gentle, and loves her like there's
no tomorrow. Or rather, I hope he finds her.
And I hope Pen and I will see each other again. If
there's an afterlife, I want to spend it with him.

I'm entrusting this diary to Pen, and have asked
him to return it to my bedroom. Bluey, if you
ever read this, I have only one thing to say: I love
you. Oh, and one other thing: if you become a
mother, take the best of what I gave you. Forget
the times when I was cross or snapped at you.
Remember the love. That's all I ever wanted to
give you, and in those moments when I didn't, it
was never about you. The failings were all mine.
Take the best that I gave you, and pass that on
to your children.

Love forever, Mum. xxxx

Six Months Later

Bluey opened to the first page of her new diary, and with a smile began to write:

This morning Clayton and I stood on the shores of my beloved Calico Bay, barefoot on the cool sand, Sun rising over the day. It was a new day, and the start of my new life. My long white wedding dress fluttered in the sea breeze. I wasn't a virgin, but I sure felt like a virgin bride. That's why I chose to wear white. I feel so young, and fresh, and new: innocent. I'm crossing the threshold to a lifetime of new experiences.

There were flowers in my hair, and I held a posy of red Kangaroo Paw flowers. I felt like the most beautiful woman in the world. Clayton made me feel beautiful every time he looked at me. Something glistened in the corner of his eyes every time he smiled at me. Olivia wore a red dress to match the flowers. We'd spent the night before painting our toenails in just the right shade of red, choosing from 25 different ones! We were fifteen years old again, giggling, laughing until we cried.

This morning I said "I do" to the man who loves me. We were surrounded by our friends and family, and as the waves lapped on the sand, I felt Emily and Pen beside us, cheering us on. My grandmother gave me away, and Clayton Lansen caught me, just like he has from the day he arrived at Bluey's Café.

Your wedding day is supposed to be the best day of your life. My wedding day has been one of the best days of my life. I've had so many best days, so many great days, and thousands of fabulous days. They're in stark contrast to the few rotten days which violated my soul and gnawed like a hyena at my femininity. Those days might howl in my memory, but they don't haunt me in the same way now. Clayton's love has shown me there are other songs; beautiful renditions to lift me to my joy. It's always been Clayton who has picked up the guitar to sing to me, but today I surprised him, and showed that I really did pay attention when he gave me lessons each day in the treehouse. Today, on our wedding day, I sang to him. There was only one song that I could possibly choose, and it couldn't have been more perfect. Everyone laughed and cried, but they knew exactly what I meant.

Oooh I don't wanna write a love song
Don't wanna let it out
Don't wanna write a love song
just in case I freak you out.
Here it comes anyway,
you can't stop them once they start.
Gonna scare you with what's in my heart.

I wanna lover that's forever
Want a cottage by the sea
Ten bouncing babies that just look like you and me
I want chickens in our yard, I want fruit upon our trees
Do ya wanna try that with me?

Well there you go, I sang it now
I wonder how you feel
Did I go too far in my musical reveal?
Feeling kinda nervous,
think I've forgotten how to breathe
Do you think that you're the man for me?
I wanna lover that's forever...

Little baby, your Daddy swept me up in his arms and kissed me, tears rolling down his cheeks.

And there, right in front of our friends and family, I felt you kick for the first time! This has been the best day. And there are so many best days that I want to share with you, just like both of my mothers did with me.

~ The End ~

197

About the Author

Veronika Sophia Robinson is an author and novelist living in rural Cumbria, in the far north of England. She has two daughters (a composer and a novelist), and is happily married to a man with a gorgeous voice. Born and raised in Australia, she thrived during her childhood on Queensland's Darling Downs. She has a great love of the Australian bush, and enjoys nothing better than an electrical storm and the scent of eucalyptus after rain. Some of her favourite things include: ripe mangos, fabric love hearts filled with lavender, lightning, kittens, hot sunshine, cappuccinos, walking in the woods, and the scent of jasmine. Veronika has been a marriage celebrant since 1995, and is a sucker for Happily Ever After beginning at Once Upon a Time. At the time of publication, she has written six novels and looks forward to writing many more. Her favourite time of day to write is before sunrise. Facebook: Veronika Sophia Robinson author

About the Songwriter

With special thanks to Mandy Bingham for allowing the lyrics to her songs *Red Dirt* and *Bouncing Babies* to appear in this novel. Mandy is a singer/songwriter from Belfast, Northern Ireland. She started writing her own songs after attending, and being inspired by, song writing workshops at the Belfast Nashville Songwriters Festival in 2012. Even though Mandy is a daughter of the late singer/songwriter David McWilliams, she never sang a note until a couple of years ago, let alone thought to write her own songs! She continues to write lots of new material and is planning to record an EP in the very near future. In the meantime, she is working on vocal training, guitar playing and getting as much live experience as possible. Facebook: Mandy Bingham Music
www.soundcloud.com/Mandy-Bingham

About the Cover Artist

Sara Simon is an artist, illustrator, writer and mother from Yorkshire. She loves trees, long walks, wild swimming, the sky, gardening, the sea, canoeing, colour, camping, chocolate, cats, and reading with a torch way after bedtime. She doesn't like cooking (except cake), driving, jazz, hospitals, or being cold.

She works in a teeny studio in a little house on the edge of the Peak District, UK, and can see the sunrise and the hills from her drawing board. Her mother encouraged Sara's creative juices to flow as soon as she could hold a pencil, and she won prizes for her art from an early age (the racing bike and healthy piggy bank were highlights).

She went on to art college in Harrogate and then a BA in Nottingham, followed by two jobs as a graphic designer. She gave up the 'office' thing to have her family, and became self-employed, working with a sleeping baby across a pillow on her lap. She lives with her husband, two sons, and two cats who like nothing better than to trail footprints across her artwork. Her home is a hive of activity, with art materials, complex lego projects, books, bike bits and musical instruments where you'd generally expect to find something else. Sara has come full circle from pencil and paper, drawing everything that stayed put for longer than two minutes; through computer-based design for print and the Internet and the high-pressure world of advertising; and then back to the drawing board, in colourful paint-stained trousers, where she says she belongs, dipping her paintbrush in her tea.

Lightning Source UK Ltd.
Milton Keynes UK
UKOW06f1946131115

262647UK00009B/119/P